Table of Contents

The Things We Dream at Night:
Modern Erotica Inspired by Gothic Folklore and Mythical Folklore

By Callixta/Calix King

A Forward with Gratitude

I never found erotica that resonated with me. I think a lot of us who are femme, nonbinary, ect have been there. Why isn't there talk about consent? Why don't we mention birth control? Why don't partners ever communicate with each other while they are "in the act"? And, weirdly enough—why is the guy's pleasure highlighted the most? Even in erotica supposedly written by femmes for femmes, there's a lack of empowerment and an abundance of objectification. It's just really strange, and books like *Fifty Shades* and even Anne Rice's *The Sleeping Beauty Quartet* haven't helped elevate the genre either.

Thus, I wanted to create erotica that had a literary feel, was charged with sensuality, and felt accessible. I found myself going back to the stories and subjects that have always inspired me: fairy tales, romantic motifs, folklore. These stories are ingrained in us. They are a cultural touchstone and, even in this modern era, remain as popular as ever. I wanted to bring that magic, wonder, and romance into my own short stories. After all, aren't fairytales the first love stories we are introduced to?

Some of these stories contain old fashioned concepts (like the act of writing love letters) while others have creatures like the vampire. I even sprinkled in a more "recent" literary figure into this collection, who happens to be one my favorite male leads of all time. With such varying characters, time periods, and locations; I wanted variety in this book—and I think I achieved that.

At this time I want to thank my amazing editors, Tyree Kimber and Averi R., for their time, skill, and expertise. I couldn't have asked for a more talented duo and I am thankful for the effort they put into making my literary debut the best it could be. I sincerely love you both and am grateful for everything you have done for this project.

I am also eternally grateful to my beta readers (N.C., B.B., and L.P.) who gave me extensive notes on their reading experience and took the time to help me. You donated your time and effort to this project when you didn't have to. I feel blessed to have you as, not only beta readers, but my friends. You helped refine this collection to what it is now.

I have to give a huge shout-out to my former roommate and friend, N.E who taught me how to market this book and made sure I drank water and ate during the final stretch. I didn't know how some hashtags could be so important, nor the power of marketing on social media. Your advice has truly been beyond helpful.

I also want to thank my two handsome partners, Jared and Patrick, who kept me sane during the writing and editing of this book. You two acted as inspiration, cheerleaders, and moral support throughout this project and I am grateful. Jared, my technologically gifted husband, you coached me well through the formatting of this ebook, and I couldn't have created this electronic tome without you. Patrick, you gave me "The Fiddler". I love both of you, so much.

Finally, I dedicate this to any queer, neurodiverse, and extraordinary human who dares to dream and create. I, as an autistic, queer, trans, femme see you. You are beautiful. You are valid. I love you and I am rooting for you.

A Note for Mental Health...

To respect the mental health of my readers, I have included a list of possible triggers and their corresponding stories. Please remember your well-being is important and, like the characters in these stories illustrate, your boundaries and needs should be respected by all. None of these stories contain any graphic violence against femmes, breaking of consent, or (unpleasurable) harm toward others. Still, other's kinks may not be your kinks, and it is never my intent to upset any reader. I hope you find this list helpful before diving into these stories.

~Callixta/Calix King

Trigger Warning List:

The Silver Illusion: a femme getting manhandled (no hurt or damage is done), a (sort of) break in, forced sleep toward one character (though nothing happens), waking up to a stranger, and a recounting of someone being violent toward a femme (nothing graphic).

Writing on the Wall: depiction of someone getting cheated on

Sheet Music: someone getting tackled, a wound with blood is depicted, consensual cursing and domination is depicted, discussion of medical procedures, mention of blood, mention of being physically sick

The Fiddler: death of a family member

The Silver Illusion

(Inspired by the legend of the vampire)
Part One:
Dorian Gray is Dead

*

"You bastard!"

The setting was stereotypical: an alley behind a featureless bar, where many wanna-be musicians smoke after a set. The time was midnight and the band, *The Haunted Stagelights*, were readying themselves to perform. The lead singer of this goth-esque band took his time, enjoying one more smoke before the show began. His smooth face appeared almost plastic-like in the pale streetlights. His eyes were a deep brown, that one could look into and drown in or get drunk on, with flat ironed locks casually falling in front of his far-off gaze. He wore skinny jeans and a velvet t-shirt worth more than what most made in a month. On a long chain a black cross hung upside down ironically.

And as he was taking a final drag of his cigarette a young woman, no more than five two, leapt forward from the shadows and punched the man's annoyingly plastic face. Trenton Lake, the victim of the night, stumbled back, his spine hitting the brick wall. His eyebrows didn't scrunch in pain, his lips didn't curl. He calmly placed his fingertips upon where the hit landed, and pulled away to inspect the blood from his broken skin.

"You're a monster," the woman said. "A monster."

He studied the young woman. Dark wash jeans, a grey t-shirt, and a pair of kick ass boots encased her stocky frame. Her hair was pulled back into a ponytail and a page boy cap sat jauntily on her head.

But looking up at him was the fire of anger burning in her azure eyes; a warning that she wasn't here to play.

1

"Eileen," he said, affecting just a whisper of a British accent. "I don't know what Riya told you about the situation..."

"Shut the hell up!" Eileen Warrick clenched her fists, stepping forward. "Say one more word and I'll make the other side of your face a lovely shade of purple too."

"You don't know everything, little girl."

She leaned in. "I am twenty-three you bastard. I am not some clueless fan that you can easily charm. I saw the bruises on her arm. I saw the emails and how you talked to her. I also saw pictures online of you making out and fucking someone who *wasn't* your girlfriend. I know enough."

His eyes narrowed at her. "*You* sent the investigator. You have too much time on your hands."

"I make time for those I care about. Stay away from her. Stay away from conventions I will be at. You step foot in my turf and I will ruin you."

"I will do what I wish," he spat. "I have more money and power than you can imagine, woman."

"I have friends in high places."

"You don't know the resources I have, bitch."

She drew her fist back again, but this time he was prepared. He caught her hand in his and twisted her arm. Pushing her to the ground, he sat on her back, grabbing her ponytail and fisting it. While pulling her hair toward him, his hand slapped itself over her mouth. Leaning forward, he put his lips to her ear.

"Don't try me," he whispered. "You are a gilded candle, a light, in this world Eileen. But I can still snuff you out."

Without hesitation, she opened her mouth and bit down on his palm, hard. He let out a cry, and in his surprise, let go. She rolled out from underneath him and kicked him in the chest. His back hit the ground with a thud, the wind knocked out of him. Eileen didn't stick around. She pushed herself off the ground and ran into the dark night, only looking back once to make sure Trenton wasn't following.

Seeing her run, he smirked and stood. He cocked his head back and forth, a cracking sound signaling a popping neck. He turned to head back into the bar, readying to entertain and charm the many who had flocked to see him perform.

Across the street, someone had watched the entire scene unfold. That someone reached into their coat pocket and pulled out a phone to check the time. Midnight was in two minutes and the show was to start soon. Time to go be a "fan". Time to pledge fake loyalties. Time to put down a rabid dog.

Knowing this was the beginning of a long process, the man in the shadows was looking forward to, and was dreading it, all at the same time.

*

Four Months Later...

Riya Chandler lounged on the red settee, her silver Acer laptop warming her thighs through her dark skirt. She was furiously typing out the final edits to her historical novel, her golden eyes glassy with the light of the computer.

She had flown to her hometown to keep her friend company as she housesat, and to complete the final touches on her most recent literary project. Glancing at the open window to her left and seeing the November snow falling, she pulled her cardigan around her for a self-given, cozy hug. She twirled a lock of her amber hair, relief sweeping over her. Her work could finally be sent off before her publisher's deadline. She stretched her lanky, tan limbs, finally unfolding herself from the laptop and heap of blankets. It was a Friday evening, the weekend was on the way, and it was time to relax. She took a moment to click through her social media; refraining from getting into debates over the remake of *Jane Eyre* as she did so. Pausing at a status, she saw her best friend's name throughout the slew of comments.

"You have anger issues Eileen," she said, turning to the blonde seated on the carpeted floor beside her. Said blonde, dressed in yoga pants and a hoodie, looked up innocently from her iPad. The two were opposites in appearance with Riya being tall and strong, and Eileen being short and curvy.

"I don't have anger issues," she said. "I'm just passionate. The woman who plays Jane has no personality. She is basically just a prop in the film! And Edward Rochester is way too stoic."

"You called Ronald Hill an overly drunk twat."

"He called me a rabid fan girl."

"Eileen..."

"I'll apologize tomorrow," she sighed.

"If you don't alienate all your literary friends first." Ri waved her hand dramatically. "Blocked, blocked everywhere..."

"Yeah, sure."

"It won't be good for your business."

Eileen rolled her eyes. "Yes, because your mother is not paying me nine hundred for two weeks to clean her mansion and water her plants, *while* keeping her daughter company and making sure she eats every now and then."

"I don't need a babysitter."

"Right. We all know how you get when you get into one of your writing funks. And for nine hundred dollars, I will do whatever your dear mother asks me to. I get to live in my happy Victorian nirvana for half a month, and have a little break away from James. Speaking of lovers, by the way..."

Riya set her laptop aside and gazed at her. "Yes?"

"Look, your mother said James could spend the night, but umm...do you think she would mind..."

"Mind what?"

"Lucas is coming into town tomorrow."

Riya took Eileen's shoulders and spun her around. "When the *hell* were you going to tell me this?"

"I just found out this morning! I tried to get a hold of you at the realtor's office, but you were with a client! They asked if it was an emergency. What was I supposed to say? 'Yes, one of my polyamorous lovers is coming in from New York to surprise me! I just found out this morning and I think I need to ask Ri for her permission to let him bang me in her childhood home since the owners, i.e. her parents, are on a *fucking cruise.*"

"Oh my god. Where is he staying?"

"Yeah, about that..." Eileen looked at Riya, her hands clasped in front of her and her eyes begging.

"EILEEN NO," Ri gasped.

"There was a reason that I cleaned this place for six hours today. Besides, your mom said I was allowed to have a partner here."

"She meant your husband, not Lucas." She sighed. "Jesus, E. I'm going to kill you."

"Can you at least wait until after Thursday? Apparently Lucas has *plans* for me. He's been so busy in New York, and he's missed me so much. I would hate to die before I had my four days of being pounded until I see God. Also he's bringing some fun toys and..."

"Jesus. Fucking. Christ." Riya released Eileen's shoulders and she shrugged. "Okay, sure, I guess he can stay here. I suppose this means I might want to stay in the guesthouse."

"No, I can stay in the guesthouse."

"I'll stay in the guesthouse. It's where my office is anyway."

Eileen sighed. "Thank you. Seriously Ri. This means a lot to me. I haven't seen Lucas in so long and we miss each other."

Riya smiled. "My family will never know. But honestly, you could probably have a satanic ritual here, and as long as the house was sparkling and the plants were alive and well, my mom wouldn't care."

She pulled the laptop back on her lap. "I'm not going to lie, I am a bit jealous though."

Eileen settled back into her iPad scrolling as well. "Well, it has been a while since...the breakup."

Riya nodded. "Maybe." She changed the subject quickly. "How's Lucas' wife enjoying the polyam life?"

Eileen smiled softly. "Well, Veronica seems to be enjoying her escapades, as far as I can tell. She didn't expect Lucas to find a partner so quickly though. That was a bit of a shock. But, I love her husband, and their child. I think when she saw that I *genuinely* cared about them, it was enough. She's become a good friend. I'm lucky."

Riya looked down at her. "I'm glad you all are getting along. I hope I can meet her next time she's in town, or we're in their neck of the woods. Speaking of our town, are you going to show Lucas around?"

"I think so. I might take him by my old school, and down to where the hippie van is overturned in the river. I'll bring him to my childhood church." Eileen chuckled. "Maybe we'll sing in the sanctuary and have a quickie in the balcony."

"That's nasty *and* sacrilegious. Good for you."

She paused. "I...I think he's going to meet my parents."

Riya pushed her laptop aside and snapped her head toward her friend. "Holy shit, you and James finally told them you were polyamorous?"

Eileen snorted. "Oh fuck no. They think Lucas and I are just really good friends and collaborators. They don't know we...*collaborate* in other ways. But maybe if they come to like him...I don't know."

"You'll need to tell them eventually."

"Oh, so you'll plan my funeral then?"

Ri sat back in mock thought, bringing her right hand dramatically under her chin. "I remember you want your body to be cremated and put in one of those biodegradable things that turn into a tree."

"I knew I could count on you."

She squeezed Eileen's shoulder. "Hey, it'll be fine. Your mom and dad love you so much. They're proud of all you've done. I think if they can accept your success and achievements, then they can also accept your idiosyncrasies and relationship orientation."

"Yeah...I guess." Eileen stood up and stretched then, a smile spreading across her face. "Okay, so I'm thinking about some salads for supper. Just a giant fruit and veggie salad. It might be good for leftover lunches. Your mom left 75 bucks just for food, not to mention what's already in the fridge..."

"I'm down with that," Riya said.

"'Of course I want a meal without meat,' says the vegetarian," Eileen giggled.

At that moment Ri's laptop pinged with a notification from her social media and she glanced at the screen. She saw there was a friend request, and she clicked on it. It was from a Kyden Knight, and everything was set to private, except for his age, cover photo, and profile picture. She tapped the profile picture and her lips parted, a small gasp escaping as she saw his face.

"Whoa," she uttered.

He was pale with sharp cheekbones, and hair so blonde it was almost white, but the natural highlights made her realize it wasn't dyed. His eyes were an icy blue, that seemed to pierce through the screen. Impulsively, her gaze moved toward his lips. They were soft and a blushing pink, that came off as expressive.

"Oh my god, *that cannot* be his real name," Eileen said behind her. Riya turned to see her leaning against the back of the settee, staring at the computer screen as well. A crooked smile lifted the right corner of her mouth. "I would totally fuck him though."

"Excuse me, *I* would totally fuck him," Riya said. "I think I'm the one with the friend request, not you."

"Hey you say he's off limits, he's off limits. I have a Tony award winning, music writing, playwright *god*, so it's all fair," Eileen said, referring to Lucas. Still, she continued to gaze at the screen thoughtfully. "It says he's thirty-two. But I would Google him first before accepting the request. He's so pretty—I don't know, he seems photo shopped to me."

Riya nodded. "Yeah," she sighed, "I remember my most recent relationship." Eileen saw her flinch a little. "I mean, mistake."

"Hon," Eileen soothed, "I'm sorry. I wasn't referring to that. Just Internet douche-baggery in general."

"I know you didn't mean it like that, it's okay." Riya opened a new tab for Google and typed his name in the search box. In milliseconds, results loaded. The first one was a website for a company called Knight Photography. She clicked on it, and a homepage with a navy background popped up. There was an "About Us" tab on the top of the website, and she scrolled her mouse over to investigate.

She and Eileen gazed over it silently for a couple minutes, also studying the pictures that were posted on the page. One was of the man they saw on Facebook, but a full-bodied shot. His stature appeared to be about six one, and while not overly muscled; one could see hints of rounded shoulders and strong forearms underneath his black button down. His long legs were encased in dark wash-fitted jeans, with black boots. A Canon camera looped around his neck, which he held gently with long, agile looking fingers. His shoulder length hair was in a ponytail in his portrait, with a few tendrils escaping. A well-fitted, midnight blue blazer completed the look, making his eyes pop. A gentle smile lit up his face.

"He should be a model," Eileen breathed.

"No," Riya said, "look at those eyes. He's—he's an artist. Meant to study and create..."

"Why not both?" She read through more of the bio. "Damn, he's been shown at a lot of galleries. The more I read about him, the more familiar he seems. I think I have heard about him from conventions. Right now he has a traveling exhibit that has to do with diversity in the comic book/cosplay world. He's written a book on photography and his recent coffee table book was a New York Times best seller." She paused for a moment, thinking. "Ri, maybe he was at a con, took pics of you while you were modeling, and he's friending you so he can tag you? Also, he's hot. Did I mention he's hot? Because he's hot."

"I would remember that face," she said skeptically. "I would have seen him."

"Maybe he took pics of you at a fashion show or a press thing then. I'd just go ahead and accept him and follow him back."

Riya clicked back over to her profile and followed her friend's command. "Thank Christ, the suspense was killing me," Eileen teased. "Maybe you can message him later this evening and introduce yourself."

"Eileen, he lives in—" she looked at the bio,—"London. I don't have..."

"Riya?"

"Yes?"

"Shut up and stop over thinking things. *Now* to food. We will talk about messaging him later." She winked. "Unless he messages *you* first."

*

The messaging never happened. As Eileen was cutting veggies for the salad in the kitchen, the snow went from being playful flurries to a full-blown storm outside. An hour later while Riya was having a stroke of literary genius, the power went out. Her laptop went black and Eileen narrowly escaped cutting off one of her fingers on the kitchen island due to the sudden darkness.

"Oh shit, oh shit, oh *shit*," Riya yelled in the living room. "I just reworked three pages of this story and I didn't save any of it. FUCK! My publishers will..."

"Yes you did," Eileen sighed. "I set up autosave for you, remember? You may have lost a few sentences, but I set it to save every five minutes. You should be fine."

"Girl, I love you."

"You'll have to fight James and Lucas for me." She paused. "Oh God...Luke." She picked up her cell phone on the counter and began texting furiously. "I'm getting a hold of my mom to see what the weather is going to be like. Maybe they still have power." She whispered under her breath, "Please let the weather be okay tomorrow, please..."

Riya used her phone as a makeshift flashlight as she walked to the kitchen. She saw Eileen trying to cut vegetables via her own phone backlight, tears glistening in her eyes. She could tell by that one glance Eileen's anxiety disorder was threatening to make her into a weeping mess.

"Eileen!" She cried, rushing over to give her a hug. She put down the knife, and leaned into her friend's embrace. "Do you need anything? Your medication?"

"No, I took them earlier. It's just...fuck. I haven't seen him in so long. Disappointment and change of plans are my huge triggers. I'm sorry."

"Hey, don't be sorry. You're allowed a few breakdowns every now and then."

"But I have to make sure you're okay. Your mother sent me here to..."

"Stop. We have been best friends for almost six years. After all this time, it's okay. You can break down."

Eileen whimpered, a few tears finally escaping. "I miss him so much, Riya. He happened to have a spare few days this week, and we haven't seen each other in five months. He's been so busy working on this production. If he can't make it, I'll be devastated."

"Hey, hey, hey. Wait till your mom replies..."

At that moment Eileen's phone buzzed, and she reached for it. She unlocked the screen and quickly read the text message. A smile spread across her face.

"Thank fuck! The lights are only out on this block and the ones surrounding it. Everywhere else in town has power. The storm should be done by early morning and the roads should be cleared by nine—right before Lucas' plane is to take off! There might be a delay, but no cancellations. He will be here by tomorrow afternoon. Maybe evening at the latest!" She wiped the tears from her face. "I'm sorry, I know, it's silly of me to get so..."

"Hey, it's no biggie. I don't *ever* have anxiety attacks ever, so I *totally* don't understand," Riya teased.

They both smiled at each other knowingly. At that moment Eileen's phone vibrated in her hand, sending out a long hum. "Speaking of my musical sunshine..." She swiped to the screen to accept the call and brought the cell to her ear. "Hello sweetie...oh hello Samuel! Now, now...did you find daddy's phone again? All right, can you bring it to papa? Yes, go find daddy! Yay, good job Sam! Now hand the phone...yes, please hand the phone to your dad please..."

Riya laughed at her friend's attempts to instruct the two-year-old, and Eileen stuck her tongue out at her. Finally she visibly relaxed, leaning against the counter with a dopey grin on her face. Riya only knew of two people in Eileen's life who could get her to relax like that: her husband James and her boyfriend Lucas. Ri was amazed that Eileen could balance two relationships so well, but they all made the dynamic work and were happy.

"Hello my love," she said, confirming what Ri thought. "The terrible twos are great, aren't they? I don't know how he could've gotten the phone off the kitchen table either. Veronica has him now? Oh yes, tell her I said hi back! Oh my God, hi V! Girl, I miss you too! Yes, call me and we will catch up sometime! Anyway, Lucas, I wanted to let you know about the weather here..."

"I'll start lighting some candles and get a fire going in the fireplace," Riya said, her voice hushed. She patted her friend's shoulder, and Eileen looked at her gratefully. She placed the phone on the table, putting it on speaker so she could cut more veggies in its light while talking to her beloved. As she left the room she heard Lucas in his delightful mid-tone say, *"Hola bonita...te extraño tanto."*

Hello beautiful...I miss you so much. Eileen and Lucas had been together for only a year and a half, but Riya had picked up on a bit of Spanish in that time due to Eileen's ecstatic recounts of their conversations. She knew the "important" things, like what *quiero estar dentro de ti* meant and *quiero cogerte.* She rolled her eyes at hearing Eileen sigh, knowing she was probably having an intellectual orgasm and would be useless the rest of the night.

Fifteen minutes later after lighting every damn candle she could find and starting a fire, she reentered the kitchen. Eileen, with a dreamy look on her face, was completing the first salad. Lucas' voice filled the kitchen. "I'm thinking about maybe going to France with Veronica and Sam for New Years. It might be nice to get out of the states for a while. We have a vacation home there, after all."

"Nice! How big is it?"

"Five rooms. Hmm, that has me thinking, maybe you could join us. It would be nice to have my other *pareja* with me for the holidays, even if it were the tail end of it. After all, last Halloween was so much fun."

"I'm going to stop you there," Eileen laughed, getting into the fridge to grab the fruit for the next salad. "Ri's in the room. She doesn't need to know all of our escapades."

"Oh, hello Riya," he greeted. "It's been a while!" Even over the phone his voice sounded so warm and welcoming.

"Hey Luke," she said, carrying a candle from the connected living room into the kitchen. "How's the family?"

"Everyone is good. V is settling Sam the Phone Stealer into bed. How are you sweetie?"

"I'm fine. I'm about to wrap another project, so I'm spending time with Eileen while she housesits my parents' place. You could say it's my mini-vacation."

"Or is Eileen making sure you eat while you finish those final edits for your novel?"

Riya laughed. "You know me too well from Eileen's stories."

"Hey, speaking of food, we need to all get dinner together while I'm in town. I do want to catch up with you. So tell me, how did things go with you and…"

"They didn't, Lucas. Mark and I decided to not go out."

"Oh Ri, I'm sorry. Daniel is newly single. Maybe I could slip him your number. He is a fan of your writing."

She contemplated for a moment, thinking of Lucas' handsome actor friend with his dark skin, brown eyes, and soft brown curls. But she shook her head. "No thanks. Unlike Eileen, I am not trying to sleep through the entire cast of your show."

"Excuse me! I flirt, but I don't do anything about it!" Eileen snapped.

"Well what about that night with…"

"I'm putting that on my Things I Didn't Need to Know list," Lucas said.

"Fair enough. Hey sugar, I have to go," Eileen stated. "The power is out, and I need to save my phone's battery life since I can't charge it. I just wanted to let you know about the weather. If anything comes up, text me, ok?"

"I will. Eileen?"

"Yes?"

"I love you."

She smiled. "I love you too, boyfriend. I can't wait to see you tomorrow. Have a good night. Give my love to Sam and Veronica."

"And send my regards to James. *Buenas noches*, my love." Eileen hung up the phone, the candlelight making her look even more radiant. Her eyes sparkled and the corners of her mouth were turned up in the most secretive, fulfilling smiles.

"Love transforms," Riya said, leaning against the kitchen island where she was cutting fruit. "I'm happy for you and Luke. You make a cute couple. Almost as cute as you and James."

"James is my special guy and you know it. But, I think he and Lauren make a fantastic couple too."

"Those two should totally have babies together."

"I agree. It's what they both want. But they are taking it slow. She just moved in with us. We will see. Now here, enough of my personal life. We have to plot you and Kyden getting together."

"There is nothing to plot about," Riya said, chewing on the apple. "As I said, he is London and I am..."

"Insanely rich and you need an orgasm stat. Look, airplanes exist. So do boats. Fuck, wait a couple years and I'm sure teleporters will be a thing."

"He may not be interested in me."

"He hunted you down your socials. He might have messaged you, but we don't know because of the power outage. Stop being defeatist. Hot London guy is hot and artsy, and probably educated and rich."

"I'm a realist."

"No, you're being defeatist because you're afraid to get hurt again."

Riya felt her face flush. "God damn it, Eileen. Not everyone is like you. Yes, the universe aligned right and you were given James and Lucas. Sometimes, the universe doesn't do that for people."

"It's not about the universe, Ri. It's about you. You're gorgeous and intelligent. You're funny and light up a room. Any guy who is smart and fucking decent would treat you like a queen and want you."

"Kyden might have a girlfriend, partner, or boyfriend."

"Or maybe Kyden doesn't and you should fuck him."

Riya smiled sheepishly and shrugged. "I don't know why you're so stuck on this, but fine. I'll message him tomorrow when the power comes back on."

"Yes, one point to Eileen. Now come on, grab two bowls and wash up. Supper's ready."

Both of them sat together at the kitchen table. By candlelight they watched the snowfall and talked about Riya's new writing project and Eileen's future house sitting and virtual assistant jobs.

"I'm going to crash on the sofa down here," Riya said, as the night crept upon them. "I don't feel like traveling to the guesthouse in this weather. It's only a yard or two away, but no."

"Hey, I can crash down here if that is the case," Eileen offered. "Why don't you take the guest room?"

"I'm not even sure I'm going to sleep yet, girly. Go upstairs and nab the room. Maybe I'll sleep in my parents' bed tonight. But you're about dead on your feet."

"Yeah, cleaning for six hours does that to you."

"Take a bath and rest. I lit some candles in the upstairs bathroom for you. Get some bubbles going. Shave. You want to be beautiful for your musical sunshine tomorrow!"

"My god you will never let me live that down!" She stuck her tongue out at her. "All right, good night, Riya. If you need anything or something happens, just come get me."

"And you do the same with me. Good night."

After Eileen slipped away upstairs Riya walked into the kitchen. She didn't feel sleepy yet and decided to reread some classic Hans Christian Andersen tales. Eileen had brought over a complete volume to let her borrow, and she thought *The Snow Queen* would be perfect for a night like this.

She placed the kettle on the stove and walked back into the living room where the fire was roaring, radiating its heat. Riya, still dressed in her clothes from that day, contemplated running over to the guesthouse to crash, since her night clothes were there. She looked outside. The snow had slowed down, but not by much. She grimaced. She would run upstairs and borrow a nightgown from her mom, rather than fight the cold outside.

The kettle screamed from the kitchen, bringing her out of her thoughts, and she hurried to silence it. Lifting it from the burner, she hoped Eileen's mom was right about the weather. She knew it would wreck her best friend if Luke couldn't make it to town. That poor woman was such a ball of nerves, and she kept it together so well. With so many people relying on her—the pressure had to be insane. Riya definitely understood that. The life of being a writer with deadlines and public appearances wasn't easy.

As she was filling a mug with steaming water, a knock from the front door made her jump. She about toppled her drink in progress off the counter, and had to steady herself. Moments later, the knocking again emanated from down the hall, and she took a deep breath. She didn't know who it could be this late at night—possibly some traveler whose car got stuck in the storm? She crept her way to the front door and opened it a crack.

Under the moonlight was a man in a long, black peacoat with white hair framing his face. He was tall, about six foot three, and held a long, rectangular parcel under his arm wrapped in cloth. In the silver light, a red scarf around his neck stood out. But it was those ice blue eyes, meeting hers, that made her brain click.

"Ms. Chandler," he said softly, his voice deep, his accent refined British. "I..."

She slammed the door in his face and ran toward the living room. She grabbed her phone from the coffee table and began to form the conversation in her head. *"Yes, hello police, this man who friended me on Facebook has found my house. I have never met him before, but he is outside my door and I think he's probably stalking me..."*

However, she tried to unlock her phone, and the screen remained black. She pressed the power button on the side. Nothing. In horror, she realized the battery was suddenly dead. Fear shot through her stomach, and she almost crumpled on the floor.

"Ms. Chandler, I am not going to hurt you!" He called gently. "Please, I need to talk to you."

She ran back to the front door. "Leave me alone!" She yelled. "I'm going to call the cops!"

"Your phone is dead," he said flatly. "Your best friend is asleep upstairs and you won't be able to wake her."

Ri's blood ran cold and she ran up to the guestroom where Eileen was staying, almost tripping on her black skirt in the process. *Oh my god, he broke in upstairs and killed her*, she thought. *Oh fuck...he killed her*. Riya threw open the door to find her friend in bed, curled up peacefully, her chest rising and falling. The windows were intact and by the light of a dying candle, she saw Eileen was clutching her brown teddy bear from infanthood in her arms, a smile on her face. Riya bolted over and shook her. "Eileen, Eileen! Wake up! Eileen!"

Eileen didn't stir, as limp as a rag doll in her arms. Ri raised her hand and slapped her across the face. Still, she didn't awake from her slumber. *What the fuck?* Eileen usually awoke at the sound of her name being called, and yet *that* didn't stir her? Had this man drugged her?

And then, Ri's stomach dropped in realization that she was stuck in her home with a maniac outside.

She slowly crept downstairs, realizing there was nowhere to go, and no one to call.

"Ms. Chandler, I'm sorry I'm frightening you," Kyden Knight projected through the door. "Please, I will not hurt you. Eileen is not hurt. Having her sleep is just one of my talents."

"Go away," she said. "There is no way in hell you are getting in here. You'll die of cold if you don't leave."

"Unlikely. Please, Ms. Chandler..."

"Get. The fuck. Out of here."

"Riya, this has to do with Trenton."

Cold passed through her body at the mention of his name. "What?"

"Please, let me in. We need to talk, you and I."

Riya ran to the stone hearth, grabbing a fire poker as a weapon. "I'm not letting you in! You'll have to break your way in if you want to talk to me so horribly."

To her surprise she heard him chuckle.

"Do not laugh at me!" She yelled.

"No, I'm sorry, I apologize. It's the...the irony that you would say such a thing. Actually, I really can't. You have to invite me."

"Are you fucking kidding me? What are you, a vampire?"

In the next moment his voice went hard, but still he retained his quiet tone. "Ms. Chandler, please, I am begging you. Please let me in."

"Oh god." She swallowed. *He thinks he's a vampire. He's insane. He's going to probably break in, drain Eileen and mine's blood, and make us into skin suits.*

"Actually, that plot is from *The Silence of the Lambs*," he said. "Now, if I was going to follow a movie plot, think more... Francis Coppola's *Dracula*. Well, just the first act I mean. I would take you out to dinner and lavish you with gifts. Biting people for the sake of blood has gone out of style and skin suits never..."

"What the hell? What the *actual* hell?" She practically screamed. "How the fuck—?"

"Mind reading is also a talent of mine," he said. "But only when you're scared. I can only read the minds of those who fear me." His voice became gentle again, coaxing. "Please, don't fear me. I don't want to hear your thoughts."

"What are you doing here?" She demanded, her voice rising. "How do you know my ex?"

"We weren't friends, if such a thing worries you."

"No, what worries me is that there is a psychopath with powers outside my house."

"I resent the word psychopath thank you very much. Listen, I know you're frightened..."

"Answer my fucking questions!"

"Trenton is dead, Ms. Chandler."

Upon hearing those words, the breath was knocked out of Riya, and she fell against the doorframe. Her world began to slow, her brain struggling to track her movements and thoughts.

"Riya, you are about to pass out." His voice was still low and smooth, but held an edge of urgency. "You need to invite me in."

Her lips parted, but her brain held back the words from escaping. The fire poker slipped from her hands, landing with a *clang* on the floor.

"Ri, you are going to black out and crack your head on the floor," he said. "Riya, let me in."

"Kyden..."

"Riya, for God's sake, let me in! Ri!" He was yelling now, but his voice seemed so far away. Her world was fading to black. "Ri, let me in! Ri!"

An intake of breath, a movement of tongue. "Kyden, come in."

She toppled forward and heard the sound of wood cracking, along with a single pounding noise. The winter air rushed in, along with footsteps. She heard something fall to the floor, something that wasn't her, and before crashing to the ground and into unconsciousness two hands grabbed her and she knew nothing.

Part Two:

Visage

*

Riya was lying on something soft, her legs and arms unable to move. Her head felt heavy, it was hard to think. There were only sensations and sounds that returned to her at first: the crackling of the fire, and warmth. Then, moments later, the evening's recollections came back to her. Kyden, the darkness, Trenton...Trenton was dead.

Her eyes shot open and she quickly raised herself. The blanket she was wrapped in fell and pooled around her waist. She felt someone move away from her on what she realized was the couch, and she looked to her right. There he was: his hands lifted cautiously, Kyden Knight. He had taken off his coat, scarf, and hat to reveal he was wearing jeans and a black turtleneck. He had pulled his hair back into a ponytail, looking similar to his online picture.

"Do not panic," he soothed. "It's okay. You fell. I caught you. The shock was great, and you could have been gravely hurt. I wrapped you in a blanket and...here." He reached over to the coffee table and handed her a mug—the one she had filled with hot water in the kitchen before this fiasco had started. His long fingers gripped it gingerly like he had gripped his camera in the self-portrait. Carefully she took it from him. She saw this time there was a tea bag in the mug, and the water was turning dark with steeped herbs. "You've only been out for ten minutes. I put the kettle back on and made you tea. Please don't panic. Can I get you some water? Or maybe sugar or milk for your tea?"

"I like it strong," she said numbly, not sure what to make of the situation. She sipped her tea, the bitterness on her tongue reviving her.

"I like my tea strong too." He also reached over and lifted another mug. "I made some for myself. I hope you don't mind."

"You're a vampire," she stated, her voice flat. "You-you can't drink tea. I mean, you shouldn't be able to drink tea." Suddenly, the realization that she was having a conversation with a vampire hit her. "God damn it...what the fuck am I saying?"

He ignored the last sentence. "Yes, yes I can. I can't have solid food, but I can have any liquid."

"Like blood."

He nodded. "Yes, like blood. That conception about vampires is true."

"Oh shit."

"No, no, no. I don't directly drink from people nor animals. As I said, biting people has gone out of fashion. Certain blood banks are how we do things now."

She looked at him in horror. "So, the blood we donate from the kindness of our hearts goes to...?"

"No. The government takes care of all that. Government workers, sometimes volunteer prisoners give blood...it's a process. It's not a perfect one, but it's a process. But I'm not here to talk about that with you."

"Yes, okay," Riya said, beginning to find her gusto again, thanks to the tea. "Fine, do tell me why the *actual fucking hell there is a fucking vampire in my house!*"

He took a hearty drink from his mug. "I would guess a woman like you would cut to the chase. I'm glad you have adjusted well to this new and earth-shattering information."

"Is Eileen—"

"Don't be scared for Eileen," he soothed. "I didn't hurt her. It's one of my abilities. She is right now having the greatest dreams and most restful sleep of her life. She will awake with her alarm, and feel totally fine."

"Promise me she's fine. *Promise me.*"

He looked at her dead in the eye, and nodded. "I promise," he said solemnly. "I wouldn't have done anything to hurt your best friend. I know how important she is to you."

She twirled a lock of her hair anxiously. "Why the hell are you so calm?"

"I'm not the one who just discovered vampires existed, darling. I have been one for four hundred years. I have become accustomed to that information." He leaned back, gazing at her. "My god, I must say you are striking."

Her mouth dropped. "Excuse me?"

"Oh, I apologize, are we still on the vampire topic?"

"No, you just barely broke into my house and we are having a nice spot of tea—yes, you psycho, we are still on the vampire topic!"

"Again, psycho and psychopath aren't my favorite words. Yes, I am a vampire, but I won't hurt you." Riya opened her mouth, but he raised his hand. "Yes, the government knows about us. Yes, this world is large and vast and there are things magnificent and terrifying. Yes, I work for the government. Yes, I deal with said terrifying and magnificent things."

"My questions...how are you...?"

"I can read your mind, remember? You're still frightened of me." He reached out, gently pushing a strand of hair behind her ear. "Ri, I wouldn't hurt you."

She recoiled from him, and a look of genuine pain ran across his face. Such a thing made her pause, and her heart lurched. "I'm sorry."

"No, don't be. I'm used to it. Or I should be after four hundred years. Seeing a pretty woman frightened never gets easier." He smirked. "Yes, I do consider you pretty. And thank you, for considering me handsome even in your fear."

Riya groaned. "Fuck mind reading."

"I'll drink to that," he chuckled, lifting his mug and taking a sip. "Ri, Trenton was one of those terrifying things that I take care of. And you were the catalyst for making it happen."

"I don't understand."

"I know. But it was your email that you sent to a few recent cons talking about his predatory behavior that...let's just say someone who knows someone got tipped off. And with that, I was contacted. When you mentioned that he was like a Dorian Gray type, things began to make sense."

Her eyes widened. She remembered those emails talking about her ex, desperately trying to contact venues and conventions letting those in charge know of his unsavory habits...his penchant to hit on teenage fans that weren't quite legal and abuse other vulnerable women. "All this was almost seven months ago. When Eileen hired a private detective, and found all that stuff out—I did what I could. I had to stop him. He really did seem like Dorian Gray."

Kyden nodded. "You have no idea. No yet, at least." He sighed. "I am old, Riya Chandler and have known many great artists. Some had mentioned a man with dark hair and darker eyes, who had a love for music yet could never possess it. So, he tried to possess women instead. There are energy vampires, Riya. He was one, who would drink on their energy to stay vital, then toss them aside. And you are one of the lucky ones that got away from him. So is Oscar Wilde." He took her hands gently. "Stay with me on this, please. Oscar was a friend of mine, a good one. He knew of Trenton—and he wrote this work to try and tell the world of his evil. Of course, Trenton had friends in high places and he wanted his revenge. I wonder if he had something to do with Oscar's imprisonment..."

"He was jailed in 1895. The timeline matches," Ri said, astonished.

"Yes, yes it does. We have tried to track him for years after he went into hiding. And almost a century and a half later, after *Dorian Gray* is published, a little email from a lovely woman in Oklahoma tips us off." He stood from the couch, Ri's hands still in his. "Come with me, beautiful. You will want to see this." She followed him, and he brought her into the dining room. On the table was the parcel he had been holding out on the porch, still wrapped in cloth.

He nodded toward it. "You may do the honor."

She unwrapped the large object and saw it was a tattered canvas, the wooden frame cracked and decaying. On bits of the canvas she saw crumbling paint, remnants of a picture gone. She held one of the torn strips in her hands. It was a dark eye, a pupil, that she knew only too well.

*

The time to strike was now.

Kyden Knight sat at the bar, peering through the hazy air to watch *The Haunted Stage Lights* perform their midnight set. He was tired of Trenton Lake's company. He was tired of being in Texas. He was tired of his mission: to befriend a man who used wealth and power to mask the ugliness that was in his heart.

He had watched him use that same power to get what he wanted with others, and he was done with it. Tonight was the time to end it all. When the band ended their set everyone in the audience applauded. Kyden clapped halfheartedly, and if he was certain that Trenton wouldn't be able to see him, he wouldn't have clapped at all.

Soon Trenton left the stage while the band tore down, and he strode over to Kyden at the bar. He ignored the women and men that stared at him who were entranced by his graceful movements. He gave his "friend" a flashing smile as he sat down.

"Have you seen my show enough that it has bored you, Kyden?" He asked, taking a sip of water that the bartender gave him.

Kyden shrugged. "I'm sorry, I'm tired tonight. You guys were excellent, like always."

"No, you're bored, I can tell. The band and I recently recorded some new songs. The cuts are rough, but why don't you come with me to listen to them? I would love your opinion."

"Do you promise to not bring any girls this time?" Kyden teased, trying to swallow the venomous tone he wanted to convey. The last time he had gone over to his house, Trenton had brought home two girls from the bar, and walked to his bedroom to show them something for "just a moment". He had left Kyden in the living room, and five minutes later, he heard a woman groan. Soon the noises became louder, until twenty minutes into what Kyden guessed was a three way, he realized he had been forgotten about. He simply left the house, his stomach twisting in knots.

Three days later he heard that one of the girls went missing. The other was found in her apartment with no memory of that night. It was in that moment reading the newspaper that he knew this had to end.

"I won't bring any girls," Trenton laughed, "I swear."

"Then I will happily join you, my friend."

Minutes later Kyden was closing out his tab, and in a small black box on the bar, he saw some matchbooks with the bar's logo on them. He picked one up, holding it tentatively between his thumb and forefinger. He closed his eyes, and took a deep breath.

I know where your portrait is, Dorian, he thought. *Tonight, it ends.*

*

Riya dropped the tattered canvas like it was a snake and stepped away from the wrecked piece. She wrapped her arms around herself, the vision of Trenton's eyes chilling her. Kyden sat down on a dining room chair, as though the heaviness of his story was physically tiring.

"Energy vampires are different from those such as I," Kyden said. "They place their essence in an object and go about their lives. As long as the object is safe, they are safe. But if the object is damaged, they are destroyed. You know what is difficult about killing an energy vampire?

The body has to be nearby. If the energy vampire is not near the object, the essence of the vampire will fly and escape into its owner's body, so that they may find another object. You have to destroy both at near the same damn time. It requires trust with bad people to be built. Such a thing can be so, so draining." His breathing became hollow, as though recounting such things made him ill. "After months Riya...I finally set a match to his portrait. And I finally strangled Trenton with my bare hands."

Ri leaned down next to him, watching him silently, her eyes shining with sympathy. "And then, with energy vampires, the one who kills them gets their memories. They feel the negative energy, feel the pain of those who they harm. I saw the women. I saw the lives he destroyed. And I saw you." Kyden reached for her, but his hand dropped short of her cheek. "I wasn't supposed to come here tonight. But after seeing what he did to you specifically, I had to. I had to say I was sorry to you. I had to say I wish I could have stopped him sooner." She glanced at his face to see glistening tear tracks on his cheeks. He wiped them away with the back of his shaking hands, and took a deep breath. She swallowed, caught off guard by his raw emotion.

"Out of all the women who he was with—you stood out to me. You stood up to him, and tried to fight back. You had the soul of an artist and the strength of a lion. You rebuilt yourself; you didn't let his darkness snuff out your light. In ten seconds of receiving his memories I knew the good and bad of you—and you were still so remarkable and lovely." Her heart began to beat faster as he spoke of her. Riya could feel as though a small flame lit in her chest, and she yearned to reach out and touch his hand...

Suddenly he laughed, pushing himself up from the chair. "Life is so cruel. In receiving those memories I almost felt captured by you. And it has been decades since I...I felt such a way...and you don't know me." He pressed a hand to his forehead. "I don't know why I am telling you this. But...I'll go. I'm sorry for all this. I just wanted you to know he will haunt you no more. Goodbye."

He turned to go, grabbing the trashed portrait off the table as he did so. Riya watched him, heat rising in her...and some heat pooling lower. She grabbed his shoulder and he spun around, her body colliding into his. Instinctively he wrapped his arms around her waist and pulled her into him. He dropped the portrait on the floor, the clattering echoing throughout the house.

With her hand to the back of his head, she tipped his mouth toward hers.

"Riya," he said huskily, "if you do this I..."

"Will what? Take me?" She teased.

He breathed. "Your mind...it's silent. You don't fear me." He put his forehead to hers. "You truly don't fear me..." He paused for a moment, before asking. "May I go further?"

"God yes."

His lips met hers, first just moving against her mouth teasingly. His tongue gently edged her cupid's bow before diving in, his teeth gently scraping against her bottom lip. She felt something sharp, pointed—fangs. She whimpered and he backed away from her.

"No, no," he soothed. "I'm sorry. My God, your mind was quiet. You weren't afraid! My fangs come out when I'm feeding or, unfortunately, aroused. You won't turn into a vampire...that only happens if you drink my blood." He smoothed her hair back. "Don't be frightened, Ri darling. Don't be frightened. I won't hurt you." He lightened his tone, trying to calm her. "Love shouldn't hurt, unless well, you ask for certain things with floggers and flails..."

She laughed, his teasing nature calming her once more. "Okay, I'm okay."

"You're shaking. How about we start...here?"

He picked her up then and gently lowered her onto the dining room table, soon climbing on when she was settled against the wood.

He pulled her to him, kissing her mouth again, his hand reaching down to caress her waist and hips. Her hands too roamed, feeling the broad shoulders of his muscles, feeling his chest contract under her touch. He was surprisingly warm—perhaps he had fed recently?

He dragged his mouth from her lips to her neck, leaving nipping, teasing kisses in his wake. "I won't leave marks," he breathed, unbuttoning the top few buttons of her shirt, "at least not visible ones. I am a gentleman after all." He kissed her upper chest, his tongue tracing a path on her skin.

"Can I, can I see your chest?" He asked meekly.

She nodded. "Yes."

He made quick work of her shirt and threw it to the floor, seeing her navy lace bra. He reached for the clasp at her back, and with expert hands he unhooked her bra and slid the straps off her arms. Her breasts were rounded, full, and tanned like her complexion.

"My god, you are glorious," he gasped. His mouth covered her right tit, and a moan escaped her throat. He let the points of his fangs gently prick it, sending shivers down her spine. Followed by his swirling tongue she felt another jolt of pleasure, and she grabbed the back of his hair and pulled. He moaned, mouth still to her breast, while his free hand reached up to massage the left one. He carefully rolled her nipple between two fingers, and from her came a delicate cry of delight.

He bucked his hips into hers and she gasped. "Oh god yes," she uttered. "Yes, yes, yes."

His mouth found hers, and his hands left her chest. He reached down, keeping his palm outside her skirt, and gently began to massage that small triangle of sensitivity. She counted the layers in her head quickly: two separated his delicate motions from her hot quim. Being brave herself she slipped a hand underneath the edge of his shirt and felt his soft skin. There was the hint of a six-pack against her palm and she high fived herself mentally her head. Sensing what she wanted, he quickly pulled his turtleneck over his head and tossed it to the floor before continuing his careful ministrations.

"There, that's fair, now isn't it," he whispered in her ear. He pulled her naked front against his. "It's...intimate, I think." His lips circled her ear, his tongue following. "I want to touch you, dearling."

"Then touch me, god fucking damn it," she gasped.

With his eyes askance, he carefully slid a hand under skirt, his fingertips skimming up her leg. He slipped his hand into her panties moments later. He glanced up at her, looking for her silent permission to move forward. She nodded. Carefully, he pressed a finger to her entrance, making sure she was wet enough, before pumping his digit in and out of her. It was as though he was keeping time with her body. With his other hand he played with her clit, gently so as to not overwhelm her senses.

"Is...is this how you would fuck me?" She asked.

He grinned, and in the candlelight, she saw his fangs glisten. "No, my darling. This is how I would fuck you."

He withdrew his hands and rolled over so he was on top of her. He pinned her hands above her head and pushed his hips into hers over and over, his hardness still clear even with jeans on. *Four layers*, she thought, moaning. *Only four fucking layers.*

"And this," he breathed, "is how I would make love to you." He stopped his movement, and then slowly pushed against her. He allowed her to feel each and every inch of him through their barriers. Over and over he stroked his length against her entrance while kissing her deeply, softly. Tongues entwining, teeth accidentally scraping against each other, still all consumed. Soon his tongue began to match the movement of his strokes, entering her when he was beginning his teasing strokes, and retreating when he placed the base of him back at her entrance. *How can this be so good, and we haven't even had sex yet?* She thought.

She put a hand to his chest. "Actually, before we go any further...and these are going to sound like dumb questions maybe, but can you get me pregnant? Do we need protection in general?"

He smiled. "Those aren't dumb questions at all. I can't get you pregnant. And I recently was tested, and I don't have any STIs. You?"

"I was tested after my last relationship and nothing came up. I'm good."

"Would using protection make you feel more comfortable anyway?"

"I am fine without, if you are."

Kyden nodded. "All right, I just wanted to check." He kissed the tip of her nose playfully. "Wrap your legs around my waist," he requested. She did as he asked, and he stood from the table, walking them both into the living room. With his strong arms around her waist, she felt protected. Even if she were to let go, he wouldn't let her fall. Soon he set her down on the living room couch near the fireplace, and they let go of each other. He lowered his hands to the waistband of her skirt, but his eyes searched for consent from her. She nodded, and he pulled her skirt down along with her panties in one movement.

"You are beautiful," he said. "You are so, so beautiful." He kissed the soft column of her neck, and then moved down to her stomach. "So warm and soft...a man could get lost in you Riya," he whispered huskily. "A man, woman, anyone I suppose..."

His breath was soon at her entrance, and he placed a gentle kiss on her folds. "Forgive me Ri...if I sip my fill and become drunk on your body." She felt his warm tongue probe her, and trail along her folds. It traced an upward path before the tip of it met her clit...and he tossed away his restraint. Two fingers soon entered her, slipping in with no resistance.

Riya found herself raising and lowering her body with the movements of his digits and tongue. He varied the pattern, keeping her on edge and her body alert. A coil of feeling began to twist in her, tightening...spinning...

"Kyden, Kyden..."

"I'm here. Relax, my dear, my queen of the night." He licked her faster, his fingers moved quicker.

She put a hand over her mouth to keep her cries silent, but her quivering body let him know she was climaxing. His movements didn't let up, but kept rhythm as she rode the waves of pleasure. Soon she stilled, and his mouth and fingers left her. He laid down next to her, pulling her close, her head resting on his chest.

"Are-are we done?" She asked.

He looked down at her and laughed. "Oh no, not if you don't want to be."

"No, I absolutely do not want to be done."

He stood from her and moved his hands to the button of his jeans. He undid it, and slid the zipper down. In seconds his pants were on the ground, as well as his black silk boxers. There he was, fully naked, and to Riya, he was everything she could have wanted in that moment. His body was lithe and toned, matching his lanky frame. His member seemed intimidating and exciting all at once. Based on his length and girth, she wasn't sure if he would fill her in the most delicious ways, or test her limits of what she could handle. He walked over to her, and laid down by her side. She reached down to touch his erection, but he gently pushed her hand away.

"You don't have to touch me," he said. "You don't have to touch me. You don't have to suck me or anything. I want this to be about you."

She let out a deep breath. He really was here just for her. He wanted to be with her, to please her. Kyden pulled her in for a kiss, and reached down to her entrance once more. His forefinger began to rub her clit, and he would occasionally slip it inside her, pumping, and then withdrawing.

After ten minutes of touching, kissing, he whispered in her ear. "You're wet enough, I think. Do you feel ready?"

She nodded. "Yes, Kyden."

He gently moved himself so that he was above her, and the tip of him brushed against her entrance. "We can stop at any time. Just let me know, okay?"

"Okay."

"I'm here with you, in this moment fully. Your wish is my command." He put his forehead to hers. "Let me know if we need to stop, or you get anxious."

And with that he pushed against her entrance, and his tip entered. She gasped. He pushed forward again, bracing himself by his forearms. He lifted his upper body so he could look at her and gauge where she was.

"Do you want me to just go in fully, or be slow?" He asked.

She took a deep breath. "On three, thrust in."

"Are you certain?"

"Yes."

"As you wish. One...two...thr—"

She didn't hear the final syllable as he shoved himself into her. There were so many sensations. She felt momentary discomfort, but he filled her so well. Despite the stretching, it did feel good. The top of his member hit her g-spot in just the right way to override the ache and make her moan in ecstasy.

Similar to the way he moved on the table, he began to ride her slowly. Each in and out thrust hit her walls and nerves in that deliciously measured way while his kisses covered her face and breasts. He left room between her stomach and his where he led her hand to her clit, urging her to masturbate with him inside her.

"That's okay?" She asked. "I don't want you to feel inadequate," he moved in again and she moaned, "because you're fucking not."

"I enjoy my partner touching themselves with me inside them. I know many who can't come with internal stimulation alone." He kissed the side of her face, and whispered, "Besides, I want to feel your pleasure."

"In what way?"

He grinned, moving to look at her as a few strands of white hair fell into his eyes. "I want to feel you come around me."

She began to gently touch her clit, and he moved slightly faster. His breathing quickened, and one of his arms wrapped around her back to pull her up for a kiss.

"My God," he breathed. "Oh god fucking damn it, Riya you feel so good."

She moved her fingers more rapidly, matching his own pace. "Kyden, I might be close."

"Do you want to come sooner?" He asked.

"What?"

"Do you want to climax sooner?"

"If you have a few tricks you want to try, fuck yes."

"Ri," he said, stilling for a moment, "biting for a vampire, while mating, can be very intense and sexual."

She looked down at him. "Okay, I'm following."

"I promise I won't hurt you. It won't turn you into a vampire. But, I want you to feel that. If timed correctly... Do you trust me?"

"Y-yes."

He kissed her deeply. "Thank you."

His lips moved to her chin, once more making a path to her throat. He stopped at her breast, his fangs nicking the side of it. "Is here okay to leave a mark?"

She nodded. "Yes, yes..."

"All right, my queen. Hold onto me."

Her free arm wrapped around him, and as soon as he felt she was secure, he began to gently lick that small space of skin. The surface began to tingle, and then moments later...

There was a sharp pain, and then another mounting feeling. She felt him gently suck at her skin, and with each tug, another shot of pleasure ran through her body. She closed her eyes, her fingers circling her clit. Suck, pleasure, touch. Suck, pleasure, touch.

"Kyden!" She cried. "Kyden, I'm close!" And then he moved faster, her fingers rubbed herself in that right way, and she felt warmth rise to the surface of her skin.

He's sucking my blood. Oh my god.

Her body shook, a scream erupted from her throat. Colors that she didn't know the name for danced behind her eyelids. Wave after wave of euphoria hit her, and with each one she met his thrusts with her own. Something warm filled her as well, but she paid little attention. She didn't know how long it lasted, but soon the waves came less, then were tinier, and she slowly opened her eyes. He moved his hips gently, taking the last few sips of pleasure away. She felt something wet on her cheeks, and she reached up. They were tears.

She looked down to see he was licking her skin. She noted two puncture marks, but they were already beginning to clot. On the side of his mouth was dried blood, hers she realized...

Her insides tightened, but not necessarily in a bad way. There was something about him taking such a vital part of her, that made her feel possessed and excited at the same time.

He glanced up, his eyes catching hers. Quickly, he lifted himself from her and wiped the blood away. "I'm sorry, forgive me. I'm sorry. You weren't supposed to see that."

"That was...it was...wow." She tried to lift her upper body but immediately fell back, lightheadedness hitting her.

"Easy," he said. "Easy, I just drank your blood. You're going to need to rest for a moment."

"I could go another round."

He chuckled. "No, you couldn't. And well..."

"Well what?"

He looked down shyly. "I came too, sweetheart. As I sucked at you, and your walls encased me—you felt so good, Riya. I'm sorry."

She laughed. "Kyden, you look like you broke my favorite vase or something. It's fine. It's actually very human of you."

He smoothed her hair back and kissed her forehead. "I'm not going anywhere. Yes, I can stay the night with you, if you'd like."

She gazed into his eyes, her mouth agape as he calmed her unsaid anxiety. "How did you know what I was going to ask?"

He smiled softly. "You were scared of me leaving. I heard your thoughts." He traced his forefinger around her breast. "I'll stay."

"I would love that."

"Actually, would you like to get brunch with me tomorrow? I can't eat, but I would love to buy you breakfast."

"You can go out in the sun?" She said, quizzically.

"Sunscreen helps. And it is supposed to be cloudy. So, would you?"

"Yes. That will be awesome. It will be nice to have a guy while Eileen has her guy."

"You mean Lucas?"

"How the hell—?"

"I work for the government, remember? It's my job to know things." He paused. "If you want, I could stay in town for a couple days. You can get to know me, and we can... figure things out as we go."

"Like rough sex?"

He laughed. "Like maybe a few dates and rough sex."

"How does dating a vampire work?"

He rested his head on her shoulder. "I don't know. Want to find out with me?"

She smiled. "Sure, why not?"

Writing on the Wall

(Inspired by love letters)

*

Excitement was abuzz in Lexworth. Coffee houses, theaters, galleries, and other artistic hangouts where wanna-be performers and creators lurked became electric with gossip. Actors, musicians, writers, artists—they twittered with excitement. *He* was there, in town. Alexander Acosta, Theater Jesus and social activist darling, was in Lexworth, Oklahoma.

And to think, it all began with a letter.

Alexander often received fan letters at his PO box in New York. It was expected, being a known playwright like his brother, Lucas Acosta. But unlike Lucas, Alexander always answered the letters personally, even if it took him weeks to get to them.

Most of his replies were brief, one-page notes of gratitude to the writers of these letters. But this correspondence was different. It was written by a young woman with the worst going on in her life, and yet, she chose to persevere. He read how, after being abandoned by her poverty-stricken parents at the age of nine, her grandparents took her in and raised her. Through hard work and determination, she earned excellent grades, especially in anything that had to do with the arts, and excelled in regional and state poetry contests.

"I feel a familiarity with you, in that regard," she wrote. *"Our backgrounds are so similar. In art, and in words, we found our salvation. After all, is that not the theme of* Secrets of a Street Kid, *that deliverance can be sought in a painting, in music, in literature no matter where we start out in life?"*

He couldn't help but smile at her reference to his autobiographical play. That show had been his baby, and the sleepless nights and hard work he'd put in that piece had paid off in a Tony Award. On opening night, he didn't anticipate that it would also resonate with so many struggling artists, like he had once been—like this woman currently was.

He read on. Slam poetry, she confessed, was more her style than short stories. Her creation came from words and rhythm, and not with fiction. Writing was her therapy, her escapism, something he could relate to. And at the end of the letter she signed her name in looping, gorgeous cursive: Camille Chance.

So, he wrote back to Camille. And then Camille replied. And then he replied. And it became this unorthodox pen pal thing. So, as time marched on and the letters went flying back and forth, Alexander made a decision.

Inspiration had struck through the world she had shown him via letter. He wanted to create a play, a series of connected vignettes, about artists creating their work and living in the heartland. His plan was to visit Lexworth for a few weeks, research the town, and conduct interviews with people. Alex mentioned this new project to a friend, who accidentally mentioned it to a relative, who accidentally mentioned it to their nephew who happened to be a journalist for the *Lexworth Post*. Soon everyone in Lexworth knew Alexander was coming to town, at some point, in October.

In the meantime, he had continued his correspondence with Camille, and had sent (what he didn't realize) would be his final letter to her. He was coming into town, he said. He wanted to get together with her—he wanted to talk to her about his new project that she had inspired. He suggested that they perhaps get dinner somewhere. He had given his phone number to her, hoping that Camille would text him with news that she had received his letter.

What he didn't know was that the letter had gotten lost in the mail and that his inquiry of, "Would you like to go to dinner?" was somewhere in Alaska. Weeks went by and he thought he'd been too forward and scared her off. He cursed himself, making the pronunciation of "fuck" into an art form, but he decided to continue the trip anyway. The little she had told him about Lexworth had piqued his interest and a show was forming in his head. Afterall, perhaps he would run into her. Maybe he could say he was sorry. Maybe, if they met, he could apologize for being too forward.

*

Camille Chance did not hate Alexander Acosta. The only thing Camille Chance was, was heartbroken in the heartland. She felt like the past few months had been nothing but a ride on the struggle bus. Even after completing her spring semester of college and having steady summer work, life wasn't giving her a break. Her roommate, Marnie Goodwin, was taking advantage of her kindness, and her boyfriend/roommate, Nick Washburn, was taking advantage of her love. On top of it all, she was working two jobs to pay the rent since Marnie had been laid off. *And* Camille was always exhausted, due to cleaning the house and taking care of various chores with their lazy asses not helping. *And* she was missing the words of her handsome pen pal playwright since her boyfriend didn't even hug her without prompting anymore.

One September evening, at the diner she worked at, Camille was helping bus a table and close down for the night. Her customers had left behind a newspaper, and the front page caught her eye. In bold type at the top of the page was: *Award Winning Playwright Rumored to be Visiting Lexworth*. Picking up the paper, she read that Alexander was coming to Lexworth. First there was surprise, then sadness, and then hope. Camille knew there was a slim chance she could run into him and maybe ask what she did wrong. Why did he stop writing? She was afraid of the answers, but she was more afraid of not knowing.

Camille wished she could tell her best friend, Leah Bell, about the anxiety brewing in her like a storm. However, she hadn't disclosed the letters to Leah. She felt loyalty to Alex first, that she had to protect him with his status as a celebrity. She knew many theater fanatics that would exploit the playwright, and she couldn't risk anyone knowing. To her, their correspondence was sacred. Camille relished the quiet companionship, even if it was through pen and ink alone.

She felt she owed Leah though, in some way, for introducing her to Alexander's work over ten years ago. If it had not been for Leah their pen pal friendship wouldn't have begun in the first place. Camille smiled, remembering those innocent, vibrant childhood days. How both she and Leah would find bootleg versions of Broadway musicals and plays online, splitting a bowl of cheddar popcorn between them as they watched enthralled. It was *Secrets of a Street Kid*, his show that debuted when they were sophomores, that inspired Leah to get involved with theater after all.

Leah, due to her work ethic and talent, would become a go-to actress for the high school and local theater troupe. She had performed locally for years, and earned leading and supporting roles in many theater productions. She modeled on the side as well, for both the stage and camera loved the auburn-haired beauty with the flashing green eyes and tall, slender figure. It was strange, how all that, stemmed from a playwright simply expressing his own story on stage.

Camille tried to refocus on the tables that needed to be wiped down in the diner, but her thoughts remained with Alexander. She was clueless as to why he stopped writing. She felt they had formed a genuine friendship during their back-and-forth letters. And perhaps...something else, an unnamed desire for companionship of a different kind, had formed as well. Camille shoved those secret feelings deep in her chest——a place in her soul where hopes were turned into what-if games, and what-if games alone. For after all, if life had taught her anything, it was that what-if games couldn't actually hurt her.

I have to deal with what's in front of me, she thought, heading toward the back to give the dishwasher a stack of plates. *I can't go there right now...I can't.*

She was trying to keep a house afloat, while trying to revitalize her relationship with Nick. She was constantly picking up everyone else's messes, both figuratively and literally. Her dreams of self-publishing a collection of poetry had even been put on the backburner. Everyone else came first. Camille tried to ignore the fatigued look on her face that met her in the mirror every morning and her shaking hands that disrupted her work throughout the day. But deep down, she knew the stress was affecting her health and appearance.

She had been honest describing herself to Alexander, and later sent a recent picture to him in one of her letters. In the photo she was posing with Leah at her 1920's themed birthday party; one of the few times she had been happy in recent months.

*

It was a photo that Alexander would come to cherish. Camille was a twenty-five-year-old beauty, wearing a black, lace dress that swept down her body elegantly, clinging to her generous curves. Her blonde hair was swept to the side, with golden curls tumbling down her right shoulder, held in place by crystal bobby pins. She wore heels that gave her an inch to her 5'3 frame, and her sky-blue eyes sparked with her smile.

When Alexander was alone in his apartment, and the isolation of being a single man in New York felt crushing, he would take out that photo and gaze at it. The image must've been burned into his mind, but still, he would look. He was a man. He was a man who felt deeply, especially when it came to human connection. He wondered what her voice sounded like. He imagined her gestures during a heated debate. In his most daring moments, he'd consider what her plump lips felt like, especially if he were to bring them to his own.

He thought about her, on and off, while on the plane to Lexworth. When he was picked up at the airport to be taken to the *Broadview Hotel* he thought about her. And at midnight as he walked by the glassy

Crescent River next to his lodgings, sleep escaping him, he thought of her. At last though, he returned to his room, and ripped his mind away from her. He went through his schedule for the next few days. Tomorrow he planned to visit a few landmarks in the area. The day after that was his first interview.

The woman he would be talking to was named Leah Bell and his discovery of her had been a fluke.

*

Leah thought it was a prank call.

She had gotten home from work, slightly tired from her receptionist duties at the *Orpheum Theater*, a recently restored venue in Lexworth. She'd tossed her purse on the bed inside her childhood room—a place she had moved back into when the theater was undergoing much needed renovations and work had been scarce. However, a brochure was lying on her nightstand. The front page read *Advent Town Houses*—and it was the complex she was moving into in a few short weeks. Thanks to her new position at the reopened theater, she was finally able to get her own place after being jobless for three months. She had even scored a photoshoot for a local clothes designer, which was helping with her deposit on the new place. At last, after being laid off, things were looking up.

Shadow, her plump black cat, greeted her as she entered her room. With a smile, Leah pet her feline familiar.

"Hello Shadow!" She greeted. "Hey baby..."

Leah was lucky to hear her phone vibrating over Shadow's purring. She quickly picked up her purse from the bed, dug through it, and found her phone. The call came from a number she didn't know, and with a shrug, she answered.

"Hello?"

"Hello, is this Leah Bell?"

The voice was familiar; a male. He had a delightful mid-tone, well-spoken it appeared, and friendly. She wondered if it was the director from the next town over, calling her back about her recent audition for *27 Reasons Not to be in a Play*.

"Yes, this is Leah," she answered, cheerfully.

"Leah, this is Alexander Acosta."

Leah stood there, puzzled for a moment, but then smirked. Her best friend Camille and their mutual pal Joseph were award winning pranksters, and this was not the first time she had been a victim of their antics. She smiled, shaking her head.

"Shame on you, both of you! Y'all are horrible friends!" She laughed. "Come on. Really? Alexander Acosta? I'm hanging up. I have to take care of Shadow."

"No please, wait this isn't a...!"

She hung up and placed her phone on her nightstand. Sighing, she scooped up Shadow for another cuddle and kiss...and then her phone began buzzing again. It was the same number, and she answered it in exasperation.

"This is going too far," she said curtly. "Look, Joseph, I am really tired. I just got off of work. This isn't funny."

"Then it's a good thing I'm not joking," the voice on the other line continued. "Please..."

"Okay fine, if it's really Alexander Acosta, send me a picture proving it's you," she said sarcastically. "I will be waiting with *bated breath*."

She hung up once more, and collapsed on the bed. Shadow curled up next to her stomach, purring as she received absent minded pets. Leah couldn't believe Joseph and Camille had called her a second time. She had been gullible with prank calls before, but it had been years since they had pulled anything like that.

Her phone buzzed with a received message, and she sighed, expecting it to be an apology which she would graciously accept. She unlocked her phone screen and opened her messages. The same number had sent her something. She opened it—and in shock, her phone fell between her fingers. The message was a multimedia one with a picture. In that picture was Alexander Acosta wearing a well-fitted grey t-shirt and dark wash jeans, holding up a piece of paper with the written words, "Can you please call me back, Leah? This isn't a prank."

God damn, the man looked as good as he had on the Tony's. His long dark hair was pulled back in a ponytail, and his unblemished tan face had a carefully trimmed goatee. His amber eyes sparkled with intelligence, wit, and humor—the things that were so common in the plays he wrote. He wasn't very tall, about five ten. However the thirty-year-old was in good shape thanks to morning runs and, in general, being a busy playwright and director.

Leah screamed. She stood up and bounced excitedly on her heels, thankful her parents weren't there to see her turn into a teenage fangirl. Leah knew she was acting well below her twenty-five years, but she wanted to get the nerves and excitement quickly, and privately, out of her system. She took a few deep breaths, and finally stilled herself to call him back.

Her body was shaking, and she sat on the floor, leaning her back against the bed frame. The hardness of the bed post gave her something to focus on as she pressed her spine into it. Sensing her excitement and shock, Shadow leapt from the mattress, and laid down next to Leah, gently placing her head upon her owner's thigh. Two rings later, Alex answered.

"Let's try this again," he chuckled.

"I'm sorry," she said. "Oh God, I'm so, so sorry. My friends pull jokes on me all the time and I just thought—God Mr. Acosta I am so, so sorry."

"Mr. Acosta is my father. Just call me Alex. I know my last call must have been a complete surprise for you. Don't worry about it."

He sounded so, so kind. The reassurance in his voice made her relax a bit. "Thanks. So um...how did you get my number?"

"I found it on your linked-in, actually."

"Oh." She felt her face flush. "Okay, that makes sense."

"Let me just jump into why I am calling you Leah. I'm working on a project. I'm writing a show about different artists in the heartland. My older sister actually found your website while we were searching for artists and she has been following your socials and blog posts."

Leah gripped the edge of the couch. "Really? Does—does she like..."

"We both think you are quite talented, and she enjoys your social media. Your acting resume is also quite impressive as well. I hope you don't find this too forward, but I have been looking at you and a few other artists from the area to discuss your experience and time in Lexworth as creatives. On October 3rd I am flying in to conduct a few interviews and visit a few locations. I wanted to know if you'd be my first interview."

Leah flailed her free arm, trying to keep her brain from reeling. "Yes-yes," she said, making an attempt to sound calmer than she actually was. "When would you like to meet up?"

"How does the fifth sound? I will be staying in Lexworth for two weeks, if that isn't a good date."

"It's perfect. I am free then." Leah had no idea if she was free or not, but she would quit her job to get that day free if she had to.

"Okay, I'm going to text you my email address. Let's set up specifics there. And rest assured, that since I am using you as a resource, I will pay you for your time and make sure you are given credit for anything I use in my project. I'm sorry for calling you out of the blue and surprising you like this. I just—haven't had the best luck with written correspondence lately, and I felt more comfortable with initial contact being over the phone."

"It's fine, really. I'm fine."

"Good, good. Leah, there is one more thing I have to ask of you."

"Yes?"

"Please don't tell anyone about our interview. I'm trying to keep this trip low key. If you have to tell your boss or family I completely understand, but I need discretion."

Leah's heart sank. The first person she had wanted to tell was Camille. But she couldn't risk losing this opportunity—not when it could open doors for her career. *Maybe,* she thought, *I could pass Camille's information along. Yes, that's it! I can work her into the conversation. She is one of the best poets in the area!* She began to bounce excitedly.

"Of course," Leah said. "My lips are sealed."

"Thank you, Leah," Alex sighed. "We'll talk again soon."

"I can't wait. Have a good evening, Alex."

"You as well, dear. Bye."

Leah waited for him to hang up first before ending the call as well. *I'm sorry Camille. I will make up for keeping this a secret…I promise!*

*

That is how Alexander Acosta ended up at the Bell home at seven o'clock on October 5th. It was a cool fall evening, a Wednesday. The residence was a two-story Victorian, painted a sky blue with charming gingerbread trim, filled with Victorian furniture and nick knacks. Some were original, some reproduction, making him feel like he was in 1895.

"I'm so glad you're here. Welcome to Lexworth!" Leah greeted as he entered, her green eyes lighting up.

"I am thrilled to be here, Leah," he said with a smile. "Thank you for hosting me this evening."

They exchanged a polite hug, before she led him through the hall toward the parlour. Her red locks, done in a single braid, ended at her mid back. She was tall, two inches taller than him in her heels. Her photos did not do her height justice, he noted. She wore a scarlet dress with a sweetheart neckline that showed off her toned figure. What he liked most about her however, were her full lips that naturally curved into a smile. It was then he realized those lips made him think of Camille's, and a pang of longing hit him in the stomach. He banished the thought.

"The house has always been owned by my family," his interviewee explained as he looked around the home. "And not much has changed since it was built, clearly. My family makes sure the necessary things are updated of course, but everything from the fixtures to doorknobs are original."

In moments, they arrived in the parlor, Alexander saw a fire was lit in the hearth, filling the room with warm red light and a cozy atmosphere. Feet away from the fire glow, on a coffee table in front of a red couch, were cookies of different kinds. Some were chocolate. Some were sugar cookies. Some had dried fruit. His stomach growled, gazing at the decadent spread.

"I was always one to have dessert before dinner," Leah said charmingly. "I actually have a stew cooking in the crockpot right now, and some potatoes baking in the oven."

He chuckled. "When I said we could enjoy dinner together I meant I would take you out somewhere. Besides, I thought you lived with your parents. I didn't want to intrude..."

"They decided to go out for dinner and dancing, so we have the place to ourselves. I wanted to give you a proper, midwestern welcome. This is as culturally real as it gets. If someone visits, they don't leave until they get a home cooked meal."

They sat down across from each other, Leah crossing her legs at the knee.

"And besides," she continued, "people talk and like to make up stories in this town. And while I love a good scandal, that doesn't mean

I want to be a part of one. Anyway, do you want some bread with some of these sweets? I did make a loaf or two, or six."

He raised his eyebrows. "Whoa, Leah. You didn't have to do all this for me."

She sighed. "I deal with stress by baking. What can I say?"

"Thank you. This is all really kind. I hope I didn't stress you out too much."

"Well, truth be told, I do have friends who plan on coming over after our dinner and interview. I plan on having them take some of this home. And don't worry, they don't know you're here! One of them has had a rough time lately and I wanted to do something nice for her. This girl needs carbs and comfort, stat."

Alexander paused in thought. "Would they like to join us? I wouldn't mind sticking around after our interview. In fact, I would love to meet them. I'm trying to get a feel for the town and the people here, after all."

Leah shook her head. "That's sweet of you, Alex. Unfortunately, one of them has a house meeting tonight, and it's going to be later. I don't want to keep you waiting." She stood from the couch. "I don't think it's going to go well for her, the poor dear. Would you like some wine?"

"Yes, thank you. What do you 'mean go well?'"

Leah sighed as she walked into the kitchen. "Well, it's roommate drama. The *hottest* gossip in Lexworth," she sarcastically, loudly proclaimed.

"Oh my," he chuckled. "Do go on."

"It's a character study, indeed. My best friend has been dealing with her housemates' shit for a while," Leah continued, grabbing the bottle from the fridge and uncorking it. "Both of her roommates have been a goddamn nightmare to be honest. One leaves things around the house, doesn't help with the chores, and doesn't contribute jack. This mooch lost her job a while ago, and hasn't found anything yet."

She carefully poured the cabernet sauvignon into two waiting wine glasses, her movements oddly punctuating the story. "In the meantime, the other roommate is, *hopefully*, the soon to be ex-boyfriend of my bestie who, in my humble opinion, treats her like *trash*. If she doesn't do something about his dumbass soon, I just might." She then reentered the parlor carrying their beverages. "It's a big goddamn mess. Camille can't do it anymore, so she's confronting the two tonight..."

Alex's eyes widened and he felt the color drain from his face. "Did—did you say, Camille?"

Leah nodded, placing the wine glasses on the table and sitting down. "Yes. I said Camille."

"Is this Camille a Camille Chance?"

She clasped her hands together excitedly. "Yes! Yes, she is! Oh my god, I love her. I've known her since we were kids. Are you interviewing her too?"

"No," he said quietly. "I'm not."

"Oh...well how do you know her?"

He leaned forward. "Has she ever mentioned me?"

"Um, well, she and I are fans of your work. She thinks you are a wonderful human being. She hasn't talked about you recently but—"

"She didn't tell you about the letters," he said quietly. "She kept our correspondence secret." He gave a soft smile. "I'm sorry; I know this is probably going to sound weird to you. But Leah, Camille and I have been writing to each other since February. She's the reason I'm here in Lexworth. Her tales of this town inspired me, so here I am. I'm realizing she mentioned you in her letters, but never by name. I'm just now putting together the pieces." He began to talk excitedly. "You're just like she described, now that I connect it all. She cherishes you so much as a friend."

Leah beamed. "I'm flattered, truly. But—but that bitch!" She laughed. "I can't believe she didn't tell me any of this. You two being pen pals—that's so cute!"

He looked down. "It felt like we *were* more than just pen pals."

Leah raised an eyebrow. "Were? What do you mean *were*?"

"It's complicated."

He picked at one of his nails nervously, but she dared to pry. "So, you know about the issues she's been having with Nick?"

He nodded. "Yes."

"You know about her childhood?"

"She grew up poor, like I did. She was raised by her grandparents after her parents struggled in poverty and then abandoned her. She keeps notebooks of all her old work in a large plastic tub in her grandparents' attic." He smiled, recalling her letters—those secrets she wrote to him. "Her favorite author is Tolkien, and her favorite poet is Sylvia Plath."

"Oh shit. You two were close."

"I care deeply about her."

"I can tell," Leah whispered. "So why aren't you two talking then? Why is everything now in past tense?"

He took a deep breath. "Because I think I majorly fucked up."

*

Leah listened patiently as Alex recounted the last seven months of letters between him and Camille. He told her how the letters began flying back and forth. In order to keep up with the response time he gave her his personal address. They had made a conscious decision to not let modern technology interfere with their literary relationship, and somehow, that decision made everything more sacred and personal. He wrote to her about his writing process, about how he and his brother would order food and get together to bounce ideas off each other.

He wrote to her about how New York, with its street musicians and moving cars, could sometimes sound like a lullaby. He would share with her his creative process, and tell her how he'd sometimes count the city lights, like stars, on the roof of his apartment building.

In her letters, she shared with him her favorite coffee house to go write at, and that she always ordered a matcha latte. She confided how she would practice slam poetry in the field behind her grandparents' house when she needed emotional release as a child. She told him how she missed writing and performing her poetry, but life was getting in the way. Between Marnie taking advantage of her, and Nick checking out of their relationship, she felt like she was a one-man island.

"Nick isn't good for her," Alex sighed. "He should be treating her like an actual partner, and standing up for her. I mean, damn it...I don't know. I don't like making a judgement call without knowing the full situation. Maybe there's more to the story and I'm just seeing her side..."

"No," Leah chuckled, "that's basically how it is. Everyone else who knows about Nick would tell you that."

"But, at the same time, I wonder if I'm just saying that because of..." He let his sentence trail off, but Leah urged him on.

"Because of what?"

He stood up and walked toward the window, gazing at the streetlights illuminating the cobblestone road. "Because of how I feel about her."

"Alex," Leah said quietly, "are—are you...?"

He turned to look at her. "I told you about the last letter I wrote, asking her to dinner. She's not interested. She would've written me back."

Leah joined him next to the window. "No, that's not Camille's style. She would've replied to you. She's not one to go quiet. And—I don't think she only wants to be friends."

"What do you mean?"

Leah grinned. "Just, trust me. I've known this girl for over ten years. It's a gut feeling I have."

She stood from the coffee table and refilled his wine glass with the bottle she had pulled from the kitchen earlier. She handed him the glass, but when he gripped the stem thankfully, she clasped a hand sternly over his.

"So, what are you going to do about this?" She asked.

"The best I can...?"

"No, I mean, seriously. What are you going to do about the matter of you and my best friend?"

He took a deep breath. "Shit Leah, I don't know."

"Well," she said letting go, "I suggest honesty, number one. She and Joseph are coming over tonight. I think if you can give her time to let off some steam with me, before I introduce her, that would be best. They'll be here in a couple hours. Maybe we can all meet up tomorrow morning and..."

Suddenly the door swung open in the hall, and Alex and Leah turned. A tall man with short brown hair and a boyish face stumbled in wearing a graphic t-shirt and jeans. Holding onto him with both arms, trembling, was a young woman. She wore a cream colored, tier skirt with a light tan pattern, and a velvet purple top. But it was his face he was drawn to, and her glistening eyes tired from crying, that still reflected a storm brewing behind blue irises.

Alexander's stomach dropped. He knew her. He knew those eyes anywhere.

"Camille," Leah said, stepping forward, "hon, what *happened*?" She turned to the young man accompanying her friend. "Fuck, Joesph what happened?"

"The roommates happened," the man holding onto her spat. "Those bastards."

Suddenly, Camille Chance looked up and past her best friend, her eyes meeting Alexander Acosta's.

"No..." she whimpered. "Not like this...not after...no..."

She buried her face in her hands, her shoulders shaking, and she slumped to her knees.

Leah's heart sank as she watched her best friend become a crying heap in the entry hall. Certainly, this was not how anyone expected the evening to go.

*

As Leah stood there, unsure of what was happening or what to do, Alex chose to react on instinct.

"Oh my God, Camille." The sentence came out of him, quiet like a breath. He hated that, even in her sadness, she was beautiful. He knew it was an emotion she had become too familiar with in the past few months. And now, he saw it looking at her in the moment: a quiet desperation. She had written about that desperation in her letters, but only now did he understand the power behind that emotion.

"Someone, please get her some water," he said, rushing over to Camille. He knelt beside her, and reached toward her. "Hello Camille..."

She looked up at him, taking a few deep breaths. Tears tracked down her face, but she composed herself to talk. "Alexander...oh my god. I never thought this would happen. When you didn't write me back I..."

He spoke gently. "Camille, I did write to you. Did you—did you not get my letter from August?"

"No, I didn't!"

He somehow never thought the note was lost in the mail. The sinking sensation in his stomach almost made him sick. Why didn't he just write again? He was an artist, used to rejection. Why did hers scare him so much?

She began hiccupping, a trigger from crying. It sounded like a squeak and it endeared her to him even more.

"I'm sorry," he said, rubbing her back. "I should have written to you again. Camille, I am so sorry."

"No, I could have written to you," she whimpered. "I just didn't want to push any boundaries. This whole thing has been unorthodox and I wasn't sure where I stood. Or where our friendship stood."

"You mattered," he reassured. "You always mattered to me." Leah nudged him, a glass of water in her hand. He took it and nodded his thanks. "Drink, sweetheart. Drink."

He held the glass to her lips, and she gulped down the water gratefully. That's when the man who brought Camille in spoke up.

"Hi Leah," he said, looking at Alex's host.

"Hey Joseph. So, can you tell me in detail, what the hell happened?"

"Camille called me and asked me to come get her from the house. She was crying, and she told me everything in the car..." he took a deep breath. "I knew she needed her best friend, and you wouldn't mind if I brought her here."

"Of course not. Thank you." She reached down to smooth Camille's hair back comfortingly.

Alex and Joseph exchanged looks. "Thank you for bringing her," he said. "I'm Alex Acosta."

"I know who you are. It's been in the news that you'd be here. I'm Joseph Griffin. It's a pleasure to meet you."

"The pleasure is all mine." He turned his gaze back to Camille. "Why is she like this? What...?"

Joseph spat the words coldly. "This is what happens when you have a psycho as a roommate and a douche bag boyfriend."

Written sentences from the past flitted through Alex's mind. "Things got worse with Marnie and Nick."

"Yes," Camille answered softly.

"I'm sorry hon. I'm sorry."

"Camille, do you want to sit on the couch?" Leah asked. Her friend nodded. "Okay. Let's move."

Alexander handed the glass back to Leah and then gently took Camille's hands. They were soft, and her palms radiated heat. Something about her fingers laced in his felt so right. They walked over to the parlor, and Alex and Camille sat on the red couch across from Joseph and Leah, who sat opposite on a loveseat.

"He's my ex," Camille said quietly.

Alex looked at her. "What?"

"Nick is my douchebag ex now, not my douchebag boyfriend." She took a deep breath. "I caught him sleeping with Marnie."

*

Another eight-hour shift at the diner, another bad tip day. Camille wanted to scream. *No one knows how to tip in this town, I swear to God.* Her aching feet made her thankful that she had a full day off tomorrow. The day after that, she was working for *Moon Dollar*, Lexworth's only decent coffee shop. She liked being a barista more than she liked being a waitress. If she could get more hours with *Moon Dollar* she would just up and quit the diner. Besides, people knew how to freaking tip at the coffee shop.

It was six o'clock by the time she pulled up to the house. She saw that Marnie and Nick were both home, and she felt her mouth drop into a frown. She almost turned her car around and drove over to Leah's, but the need for this house meeting to happen won out over her desire for a calm environment. She had to confront them about the money problems and the lack of help with chores. As she exited the driver's side, she had to fight every instinct to not check the mailbox. Alexander hadn't written her back in over a month. She knew she wouldn't hear from him again. The kind words from him were gone like childhood days, like popsicles melted under a summer sun.

Camille unlocked the front door and, to her surprise, walked into silence. Usually, Nick was in the living room playing video games, or Marnie was blaring music loud enough for the neighbors to hear. However, this evening, there was stillness. Until she heard a woman's moan.

And then another, this time from a guy. A guy who sounded like Nick. Camille knew this specific moan only came from one type of activity—and she felt bile churn sourly in her stomach. She crept toward the currently closed room Nick and her shared, and the noises grew louder. Anger overrode her anxiety, and she swung open the door. Thus, Camille's worst fear was confirmed.

There, in the queen-sized bed *she* had bought, wrapped in the sheets *she* had purchased, were Nick and Marnie doing the sideways tango. Marnie's short, mousy brown hair was tangled; with her eyeliner running down the corner of her eyes, making her look like a raccoon fresh out of a garbage can. Her thin arms were wrapped around his, holding on for dear life like he was a roller coaster. Nick's toned body was completely naked, his hands clasping Marnie close to him. His dark hair was sticking up every which way, and his blue eyes (the ones that first caught Camille's attention two years ago) were wide with shock. They both stared at her, not moving from their positions.

The tears didn't come. Oddly enough, there was relief. Camille had suspected for a month or two that this was going on. Between the hickies that were showing up on the single Marnie's neck, how often *both* were absent in the evenings and nights, and Nick's loss of interest in Camille, she had wondered...

She felt exonerated. She felt validated. The space between her and Nick existed—she hadn't made this all up in her head, like Nick insisted.

"Baby we do talk," he reassured when confronted about him being distant. "Don't I take you out once a week? Don't I text you every day?" Weirdly enough, Alexander popped into her mind in those moments.

Sweet Alexander, who spoke to her in letters and communicated through pen more than Nick ever did. The feelings that had budded since her and Nick had been growing apart—she didn't have to feel guilty about them anymore.

"Fuck you both," she uttered, staring at the pair. "And—thank you. I can leave this situation without feeling guilty. Seriously fuck and thank you." She turned to leave her room, but lingered in the doorway for a moment.

"It's not—it's not what it seems," Nick said.

"Shut the fuck up, Nick," she hissed. "Let me tell you how this is going to work. I want both of you gone between two and six tomorrow. I will grab my things then. I want off the lease without a fight. You'll take over payments for everything."

"That's ridiculous!" Marnie screeched.

"You are not in a position to negotiate anything with me, you backstabbing bitch. Since you just got a job and don't have any pay check history, you wouldn't be able to find a place to rent anyway. I am doing you both a favor by moving out." She glared at them over her shoulder. "Seriously, fuck you both. You two deserve each other."

Camille moved her hands behind her back and untied her diner apron, letting it drop to the floor like a curtain signaling a closing act. And then, she walked back outside. She pulled her phone out with shaking hands and dialed the friend that lived closest to her: Joseph.

In three rings he answered. "Hey Cam, what's up?"

"Yeah, um, Joseph...are you free now?"

"Leon and I just got done with our date at the café. What's going on?"

She kept her voice steady for one more sentence. "Joe, I need you to come get me." And then, she fell to her knees on the driveway, and broke down into a sobbing, tear streaked mess.

*

Alexander held her close to his chest as she filled him and Leah in. She kept her voice even throughout the entire story, but the pain in her eyes told him all she did not say. She was furious. She was hurting. And she did not know what the next step was.

"That son of a bitch," Joseph uttered. "I never liked Nick Washburn. He just looked like the cheating type."

"*Es una canción de puta,*" Alexander said. "That's all he will ever be. No man who cheats is a real man."

"Everything feels overwhelming right now. I didn't quite think things through with the whole moving out fast thing." she admitted. "I have to figure out where I am going to go."

"Camille, move into the townhouse with me," Leah suggested. "I was going to turn one of the bedrooms into an office, but I can make a corner in the basement be a space for my desk. Until you move, I am sure my parents wouldn't mind if you occupied the guest room. They love you and would totally understand."

"I would be happy to move in with you," Camille said, smiling for the first time that evening. "But I know you don't move in for another three weeks. I can't have your parents housing both of us. They've done so much for me as it is."

"I'll help you look," Alex offered. "We'll find a hotel or AirBnB."

She looked up at him, placing a hand on his arm. "Thank you, but I can't. I just paid rent last week and can't afford to do something like that. I was thinking I could go to my grandparents' or something..."

Leah inhaled, sharply. "They are an hour away from your jobs, Camille! That would be *ridiculous*."

"And *I* will pay for your accommodations," Alex said. "You shouldn't have to go back into the space where you got cheated on. None of this is fair to you."

"I can even help you pick up your things," Joseph said. "We may have to come back for the bigger items when you move in with Leah, but Leon and I can do that on our own if need be."

She shook her head. "I appreciate all of this, really. I don't want to put anyone out. Alex, I know you're here researching for your new show and…"

"And I can book my room for another week. I can stay longer. But your situation needs to be handled now."

"He's right," Leah said. "You always help out others, Camille. Karma is allowing you to cash in this time."

Alexander placed a hand under her chin and turned her face up to his. "I have considered you a dear friend for the past year, Camille. Please, let me help."

She nodded. "Okay. But I will pay you back."

"I am not hurting financially my dear. To make up for my silence, let me be kind to you." He reached up and smoothed back a stand of hair from her face. "You deserve this, *princesa*."

For a while, Camille only looked at Alexander, warmth spreading to her cheeks. and then, Joseph cleared his throat.

"I say, we discuss this over dinner," Leah suggested, standing from her seat. "Joe, I know you ate, but you're welcome to stay for dessert."

"I will never say no to free dessert," he chuckled, following her to the dining room.

Alexander and Camille both stood. They walked behind Leah and Joseph, so no one else saw Alex as he reached over and took his *princesa's* hand.

*

For the rest of the evening Joseph, Alex, Camille, and Leah ate together, drank more wine than they should have, and discussed the nature of theater, the power of words, and (in Camille and Alex's case) played catch up. What the two pen pals didn't know was that they would get caught up in their own conversation and forget that Joe and Leah were sitting there. The two friends would just look at each other knowingly, smile, and then make some teasing remark at being forgotten. However, as Leah observed them interact, she realized she was watching two people fall, at the very least, in very strong mutual like.

When Leah's parents arrived home later, they insisted that Camille at least stay the night. They greeted Alexander warmly, and also said he was welcome to stay as well. It was almost midnight, and luckily, the house had a spare guest room and a pull-out couch. Joseph, since he only lived two blocks away, walked home after Leah's parents returned, saying he would pick up his car in the morning. However, Leah, Camille, and Alex stayed up in the living room, enjoying the warmth of a newly lit fire, and talked late into the night. Finally, at 2 AM, Leah stood from the couch.

"I have to crash y'all. Some of us have work in the morning. I think Mom laid out a nightgown for you in your room, Camille."

"Yeah, I should probably sleep too," Camille said. "I will leave a note for your family, saying to not worry about breakfast for me. Your father always tries to make a banquet when I'm here..."

"Well, I am taking you to breakfast tomorrow anyway," Alexander stated.

She smirked. "Oh, are you?"

"I have to do research on the town. So, someone should direct me to the best eatery, no? And research is no fun to conduct alone."

"Well, I suppose I can help the great playwright, Alexander Acosta, in his latest artistic endeavor," she said with mock drama.

"So, it's settled then," he chuckled.

With a final round of good nights, everyone at last made their way to their separate quarters. Camille took a quick shower and then slipped on the cream-colored nightgown Mrs. Bell had placed on the bed for her. She laid down and tried to sleep—but the world of velvety blackness eluded her. She felt wired, as though her body was buzzing. After about a half hour she finally got out of bed and decided to take a stroll on the wrap-around balcony.

She grabbed a red fleece blanket from the edge of the bed and wrapped it around her shoulders for warmth. After slipping on her ballet flats, she left the room, and walked to the end of the hall, where a door led to the balcony. She pushed it open and turned to her right. To her surprise, looking up at the moon with his hands in his pockets, was Alexander.

Hearing her open the door, he looked over and smiled. "You couldn't sleep either?"

She shook her head. "Too much has happened today."

"That's totally understandable."

"Why are you up?"

"I have two characters in my head fighting for my attention. I jotted down a few notes, but I really can't get my plot fully out there until I'm in front of my laptop. Unfortunately, it's back at the hotel."

"We don't have to get breakfast tomorrow if you want to write."

"Eh, they can wait until I'm free again."

She paused in thought for a second. "You know, if you want to write together, I have my own notebook in my purse. I carry one with me everywhere I go. If you want to pick up your laptop before breakfast, I am not against brainstorming with you."

He smiled. "I would really like that, actually."

She walked over to him so they were standing shoulder to shoulder. They looked out at the night sky, studying the stars like glitter against a velvet backdrop, the crescent moon shining like a florescent smile.

"I missed you," Alexander said suddenly.

She glanced at him. "What?"

"I missed you. I should have written you. I just thought—maybe I was too forward in my last letter. Maybe in asking you to dinner, you thought that I had less than noble intentions in mind."

"I wouldn't have thought that about you."

"And I should have known that. I was just so afraid to write you again. It's amazing, how I am a man who makes his bread off of words and has faced rejection repeatedly, and I couldn't bring myself to write again—to possibly face rejection from you."

She leaned against his side. "It doesn't matter now, Alexander. It's alright. It's okay."

He wrapped an arm around her. "You know, you are as delightful as I thought you would be. You have a poet's heart. You really do speak all in your words; straight from your soul to the page."

"I have to hide myself in the real world every day. I don't want to hide in my writing. In many ways my correspondence with you was more honest than many of my relationships."

He sighed. "Camille, I am sorry about what happened with Nick today."

She shrugged. "It is what it is. Honestly, this has been coming for a while. We just—stopped talking. He thought his video games were more important than our relationship, and he found his needs met with Marnie I suppose." She paused. "It's partially on me. I don't have a lot of experience in relationships. He was only my second one. I knew something was wrong, and I kept trying to get him to communicate, but he wouldn't. I just didn't want to fail."

"None of this was your fault. I know you tried. You told me how hard you tried in your letters. You did the best you could for what you knew at the time."

To his, and perhaps her own surprise, she said quietly, "I knew it was ending when I saw you cared more about me than he ever did—and when I started caring more about you than I did him."

She turned her face to look up at his. It was then she saw he had been gazing down at her, a soft smile pulling at the corners of his mouth. His eyes held warmth and an adoring playfulness in them. There was something so pure about his gaze, something so sweet—

That she kissed him, right then and there. It was a gentle, quick peck on the lips. Realizing what she did, she backed away from him, her hands over her mouth.

"I—I don't know where that came from," she gasped. "I'm sorry. I just met you today. You—you must think I'm a stupid fan girl, some sort of crazed theater..."

He interrupted her. "My god Camille I have been wanting that for months."

And then he wrapped his arms around her and kissed her, this time deeply. She couldn't remember the last time she had been kissed like this. His mouth moved hungrily against her own, the tip of his tongue tracing the outer edge of her lips. They parted, and soon the kiss became wet, hot, and wanting. But still, his hands remained gentle, one keeping a hold of her waist while the other ran through her hair.

They at last backed away from each other, him giving her a sweet peck on the cheek as he did so.

"Ms. Chance, will you spend these two weeks with me?" He asked. "When your off work, and I am not doing research for my show—"

"Like you even have to ask," she said. "But what if this continues to go well? What if this," she motioned between them, "isn't a fluke?"

"Then I guess you'll just have to let me fly you to New York regularly."

She smiled. "I guess so." She took his hand. "Come sit with me?"

"Where?"

"I'll show you."

She led him to the back section of the wrap around balcony, where it overlooked the garden. With cooler weather approaching things weren't as wild and green as they usually were, but there were still some marigolds, snap dragons, and other flowers here and there hanging on for dear life. And the moonlight made everything look like there was a cool silver filter over it, as though there was a magical haze over the ground.

"This place looks enchanted," Alexander said.

"Some say it is." Camille motioned toward a white wooden bench that was placed near the railing. He sat down first, and as he did so, playfully pulled her with him so she was sitting on his lap. She let out a cry of delightful shock and wrapped her arms around his neck. His lips caught hers again—and this time he dragged his mouth from hers to the soft column of her throat. She felt the tip of his tongue tracing her skin, and soon she noted the pressure of his roaming hands. His palm slid up her waist, stopping short of her breasts.

"Is this okay?" He asked.

"Yes."

"Are you sure?"

"Alexander, I haven't had anyone touch me like this in months, and honestly—I used to dream about you doing this to me."

"Well then, I'm honored."

She grinned. "Don't tell me you are honored. Show me what you can do with that gumption."

"Gumption? What an antiqued word."

She leaned into him, her mouth hovering above his.

"Words are timeless and I am a writer. Words are like wine to me. The older they are, the finer they are. Words like *sexus, guadens, diligitis, pragma, agape, eros...*"

"I know those words."

"Do you?" Her tongue crept out and licked the edge of his upper lip. "Then show me you know."

He kissed her fiercely, and her hands moved low to run across toned chest and stomach. To his surprise she found the edge of his tee and pulled it over his head, revealing his smooth, lean build.

She glanced at him for a second, a smile flickering across her face, before curling close to him to mouth his shoulder playfully.

"Careful," he chuckled. "We are guests in this house. I think it would be a little disrespectful for us to bone on the balcony."

"Fair enough. I do feel a bit like a teenager, quietly making out in a hidden place, hoping we're not discovered."

She looked at him longingly, and his eyes reflected the same hunger. "I have an idea," he said. He moved from his seat next to her to kneel down in front of the bench. He placed his hands on her waist, and gently pulled her forward to kiss her. "Do you trust me?"

"Absolutely."

"Okay. Tell me if you want to stop." His fingers found the bottom of her night gown, and he pulled the skirt up to expose her knees. He adjusted himself so his body was in between her legs, yet he left room for his fingertips to trail up the inside of her thighs. With the fabric of her gown and blanket over his hands she couldn't see what he was doing, but that only heightened every sensation. His dark eyes watched her, carefully gauging her reactions. God, she felt like she could drown in those amber irises. She fought back a smile, knowing that when he reached the most secret part of herself, he would find out she wasn't wearing any panties.

His index finger brushed against her folds, and his mouth dropped. She burst out laughing.

"I'm sorry, I should have warned you," she giggled. "But the look on your face is priceless."

"I'm not offended," he said, smiling. "Let me guess, you don't wear panties to bed?"

"I'm usually sleeping alone, so no."

His brow furrowed. "But you had a boyfriend."

"Alexander, the relationship was long dead before the official breakup today. He was either working, or apparently, sleeping with Marnie."

"Oh my god, Camille..." She put a finger to his lips.

"No more sad things. I want us to feel good about each other tonight."

He smiled. "I want *you* to feel good about *yourself* tonight. And let me start off by saying, my god, you are sexy."

"And you are sexy as well."

"Would I appear sexier if I said I didn't wear boxers to bed?"

She smirked. "Kind of."

"Yeah, fair enough. It's sexier that you don't wear panties to bed."

"Hey, I bet it would be amazing if, maybe some time, we both didn't wear under things to bed."

"That is a genius idea. Now," he began to teasingly trace his fingers along her folds, "I think I was about to finger you until you came."

"No one has ever been able to do that."

He leaned in and whispered in her ear. "Challenge accepted."

While his fingers explored her tentatively, his free hand reached up to cup her breast. He looked down at her lap, the fabric of her skirt pooled there, covering her thighs, the only hint that his hand was there being the subtle rustle of the nightgown with his ministrations.

"Don't you want to see what you're doing?" She asked.

He looked at her. "That's part of the fun of it. I'm not here for my own visual feast. I am here for you. So, what do you want me to do right now?"

"I want you to take your hand away from my chest, pull me close, and kiss me while you're touching me."

He did as she asked in one, quick motion. His hand pressed itself to her back, pulling her so she was almost chest to chest with him. He left space between their lower bodies for his hand to work, and within moments of kissing her; she was wet enough that two of his fingers slipped inside of her with no resistance.

Her mouth parted from his to let out a gasp as his fingers curled upward to rub her g-spot. She buried her warm face in his shoulder, his skin cool from the night air. He turned his head so he could still kiss her neck and ear; while whispering raunchy deeds he wanted to do to her in Spanish. *"Quiero metértela. Voy a devorarte. Te gustaría eso, ¿no? Si sigues gimiendo así, te llevaré a este banco ahora."*

He nibbled at her ear and her toes curled. God damn, she couldn't remember the last time she felt like this.

His thumb began to massage her clit as his fingers continued to pump in her. How did he get so good at this? *How?*

"Alexander, kiss me," she begged.

"And why should I do that?" he teased.

"Because I am going to come soon and I'm a screamer."

Without another word he did as she asked, and soon, she clenched around his hand and he felt a cry vibrate from the back of her throat. Moments later she stilled, and his lips parted from her. He withdrew his hand so he could hold her in both his arms, and she quietly laughed.

"That—that was something."

"It was," he agreed. "That was fun." He turned back to gaze at the garden. To his surprise, the pink of the sunrise edged the horizon. "Well, so much for sleep."

Camille shrugged. "No one remembers the nights they got plenty of sleep."

He grinned. "Fair enough. Let's catch a nap later?"

"My place or yours?"

"Well clearly my place."

"Only if we can just cuddle."

"Just cuddling sounds nice."

"Alex, I think this is the beginning of a beautiful friendship."

"I was hoping for more than that, Humphrey Boggart." He kissed her forward. "But here's looking at you, kid."

Sheet Music

(Inspired by *The Phantom of the Opera*)
Part One:
Shadows and Sheets

*

It had been fourteen years since David Kynaston, his kind mentor and director at the Grand Guignol, had given Erique work as a stagehand. The aging thespian had found him after chasing away a group of young men, who beat upon a thirteen-year-old orphaned Erique. His future mentor tended to his wounds, gave him water to drink, and bought him dinner. During that meal, in the light of the pub where they dined, David saw the scars—the thing that made many shrink away from the boy. After hearing how Erique had been abandoned as a child and was still in the streets, David offered him a place to live, a job, and his first glimpse at human kindness. That was how Erique, with no known last name, came to live under the stage of the horror theater, hidden away from the world and its cruel gaze. Of course, he almost couldn't blame them for looking. He was an animal, an abomination. His strangely pale face, black hair, and deep scars on the right side of his face confirmed that to the outside world. Perhaps that was why he felt at home in a theater that created scares in a proscenium arch.

Many within the theater thought the scars could be attributed to a machinery accident. Most didn't ask, only stared. However, to those who dared to look beyond the disfigurement, he was not all strangeness and ugliness. His dark green eyes held a lofty beauty to them; those deep emerald pupils that sometimes shone with poetry and intelligence. He had an expressive mouth which could build one up with literature or tear them down with the most brutal of curses. His knack for knowledge, his ability to learn at an astonishing rate, was a skill he built up himself. While he had no mother, father, or teacher—he possessed a brilliant mind he had been blessed with at birth.

Erique leaned against the wooden railing, gazing at the scene below him. Suddenly the lobby doors burst open.

"Stop rehearsals! Stop!"

An elderly, lanky man with the energy of one half his age ran down the aisle of the audience, and leapt on stage.

"What the hell?" David yelled from his director's seat. "Leo, what is the meaning of this?"

Leo smiled, holding his arms wide. "Charlotte DeLaney has added us to her tour stop. She will be performing for a week with us!"

The cast and crew let out a chorus of surprised cries, and then the questions came.

"Christ, really?"

"Surely you jest?"

"We have *her* on the bill?"

"Oh my god, oh my god...but how?"

"Now, now," Leo proclaimed, "give me a moment to talk! The manager received a letter saying she wanted to perform here. She apologized for the short-term notice, but when she received word that our theater was still here, she said she felt she must!"

"Why though?" David asked, rising from his chair. "She's performed in opera houses. She's known worldwide. She doesn't need the money."

"Only desperate performers come here!" An actor laughed.

"She said this place means a lot to her. Apparently, she started here as a costume girl and—well someone discovered her. The rest is history." Leo hurried onto the backstage, laughing. "Christ, Charlotte DeLaney, performing here. Who would have thought?"

Erique witnessed the hubbub quietly, his hands tightening on the railing. Charlotte DeLaney? She was coming here, to this rundown, pulp theater? He smiled. It was her that he first heard on a gramophone, the wax cylinder producing her melodic and haunting voice. He took a deep breath. If one could become intoxicated with a voice, then hers had been the one to entrance him. He would often sneak away into the costume room and listen to her through that scientific marvel that was kept up there. He had probably memorized the entirety of *Faust* by now thanks to her and was thankful the wax hadn't become completely worn.

"Charlotte DeLaney." He tested her name upon his lips and another rare smile left him. He would be backstage, helping make magic for her. He let his thoughts wander, painting pictures in his mind of what she could look like. Was she like the more seasoned divas of the opera, primmed with the latest fashion like a decadent peacock? Or was she more reversed, preferring some privacy in her everyday life? He couldn't wait to gaze upon her. He would experiment with the gaslights and discover how he could make her shine upon the stage. No matter the age or appearance, with a voice such as hers, she deserved it.

He bolted down the catwalk stairs and below the stage, listening to the clamor above him as everyone hurried about. Others were laughing, women were giggling, divas were jealous. He, for once, joined them in their joy.

Later that night he made the usual rounds. He lived in the theater, away from the prying eyes of the world, underneath the orchestra pit. He always checked the gaslights before going to bed and made sure the flies were tightly secured. This was his space after all, and he protected and cherished it as *his* home. Erique began on the top floor, making his usual checks in the costume and prop rooms. As he walked around, he hummed *Faust* and replayed the music in his mind. DeLaney's voice captured the innocence of Marguerite, yet still, there was a gentle power that only a unique voice and woman could possess. An hour passed and soon his nightly duties were completed. He walked back to the costume room and shut off the gramophone. He then moved downstairs so he could gather his black great coat, and go out to buy a few items from the night market. If he kept the hood low, no one ever stared at him.

And then, right before he reached the door of his abode, he heard footsteps on the catwalk and stopped. It took only a moment to spring into action. He bolted to the stairs and bound up them two at a time. In the dark he could see the outline of a young man, a few inches shorter than he was.

"Stop!" He cried. "Who are you?!"

The figure turned to look back, and then he ran. Erique bolted after him. To Erique's surprise the man turned a few times, sliding between the railing to fall gracefully to the second catwalk below, landing on his feet. Erique's eyes widened. This person knew the theater well, whoever they were. But he was quick too, as he caught the young man on the stairs just before descending to the stage. He grabbed the man by his shirt sleeve, and he heard it rip.

Erique tackled him, soon pinning him down with his knees. He took a match from his shirt pocket and quickly lit it. He moved it close to his captive, while trying to keep most of the light away from his scarred face.

"Now we will know who you are—" He growled.

But he stopped short. What he saw wasn't a man—but a woman in man's clothing.

She was beautiful, her blue eyes wide with fear, but the rest of her face didn't show it. She breathed through plump, pursed lips. Now in the light, could he see her curves through a tweed vest and a now ripped white button down. Her golden hair was tucked into a page boy cap haphazardly, a few curls freeing themselves from the cap's hold.

"State your name," he commanded, trying to keep his voice level.

"I apologize," the woman said, her voice clear as a bell. She enunciated her words carefully, and while her accent was American, she still had a slight—what possibly could be—an English pronunciation of some words. "Please, I didn't mean to startle you."

"I wasn't startled. My job is to keep thieves and trespassers like yourself out of this theater."

"I am no trespasser."

He raised an eyebrow. "Well then, who are you? You try my patience."

She swallowed. "I am Charlotte DeLaney, and I am only here to visit at my old home." Her composure dropped with a sharp intake of breath. "I am to perform here in a few days' time. But... I.."

"No," he said in disbelief. She looked young; she couldn't be more than twenty-five. "Impossible. If you are Charlotte DeLaney..."

"I know. I was not to be here until next week. I have come early, from England. My tour there has been cancelled. We had a legal issue with one of the contracts and..."

"And you come here dressed in men's clothing, why?"

She raised an eyebrow. "Do you really think a woman such as myself could safely walk these streets at night? Now," she looked at his body above her. "Since this is settled can you...?"

"How do I know you're not some other street urchin come to murder me and make off with our money box?"

She smirked. "Fair enough. If you know my voice, I can prove my identity with my singing."

"Then, sing."

"I need you *not* to be crushing my lungs first."

He rolled off of her, and she stood. Walking a few feet away from him, she took a few deep breaths, and then turned to sing a few scales. That voice...oh god. Strong tone, the vibrato controlled. She sang from her diaphragm, and her volume and pitch were on point. He had only heard such a tone from his precious wax cylinder and gramophone.

"Charlotte," he whispered. "Forgive me, please forgive me..." He looked at her in awe, his hands raised apologetically...when he noticed her shoulder was bleeding. "You're injured."

"It's nothing...."

"No, it needs tended." He helped her sit up and examined her wound. It was a gash, but nothing that was deep or severe. He thought it had probably occurred when he tackled her to the ground. "I fear this was my doing. I apologize, Ms. Delaney. Please, let me dress your wound. Are you comfortable following me under the stage? I have bandages down there." He had learned from his years at the theater it was best to keep some medical supplies on hand. Accidents, especially in the catwalk, were more common than anyone cared to admit.

She nodded. "All right."

"Come with me," he whispered, walking away.

Erique looked back, making sure she was following. He opened the trap door stage right, and he entered first. He looked back, and motioned for her to descend next. She looked at him cautiously.

"The stairs are steep. I want to be able to catch you if you fall," he explained.

She nodded. "Well, we shall carry on then."

She felt for the railing in the dark, and was able to maneuver successfully across the stairs without faltering. However, on the last step, she knocked her injured shoulder into a beam and the pain made her stumble. He turned and wrapped an arm around her waist, saving her from a tumble.

"Son of a poxy whore, that beam didn't used to be there!" She cried.

His eyes widened upon hearing her refined voice say such crude vernacular. He smiled, as he helped steady her on the base of the steps. "What do you mean when you say 'used to'? That implies that you knew this theater well."

"I was a costume girl here for five years," she explained.

"We learned this morning that you used to work here, but I couldn't have guessed to that extent. You seem so...refined. Most here aren't exactly the upper crust of society. How did you end up here?"

"My parents were business people. My mother was a seamstress; my father ran the financial side of things. We fell on hard times and relocated here when I was eight. I had to leave my schooling and find work. The old costume mistress offered me a job here, asking if I could be her assistant due to my mother's experience, and I said yes."

Passing through an entryway, they entered his abode. Through the dark, he led her to his cot, and set her down upon it.

"Give me a moment, I need to turn on the gaslights."

He moved to the lanterns he had hanging on the wall, and turned the switch to light them. In moments, his humble home became illuminated. Erique waited before turning to face her. With studying eyes, she took in the shelves of books that covered the walls and his chest that held his few belongings. His cot was nestled tidily in the corner of the room, along with a wooden box that had a ceramic wash basin and pitcher on top of it.

He took a deep breath, readying himself to turn to her in the light, and expose his face. "I must warn you of my appearance," he said. "Please, don't be frightened. I will only tend to your wound and then you may leave. I will not accost you."

"My first job was in a theater that created horrors. Nothing you can do will shock me."

He smirked. "I'm real, unlike everything else in this place. I hope you do not possess a delicate system."

"My system has never shut down from such base things as appearances." Slight annoyance seeped out in her tone. "Turn to me."

He did as she asked. He could see her face perfectly clear now, due to the lighting. She had taken off her cap to reveal her blonde hair tumbling down to her mid-back, and she was twirling a curl around her finger. Seeing him, she dropped her locks, and touched her fingertips to her mouth. Even with wide eyes, she did not cry out or look away.

"I give you credit for keeping your composure," he said, walking toward his chest at the end of the cot. He opened it and pulled out a clean washcloth, as well as some bandages. He also retrieved a whiskey bottle that was such rot gut that the cast only used it for cleaning wounds.

"This is going to sting," he said, opening the bottle and tipping a little of the liquid on the rag. "May I sit next to you, or do you prefer I stand?"

"You may sit with me," she said.

He moved slowly, to avoid startling her. Those studying eyes in turn followed his movements. With her upright posture and pursed lips, she appeared to him to be like a female bird guarding her nest, her space—if the bird had been a phoenix.

He situated himself next to her, his fingers brushing her skin as he peeled back her shredded sleeve to touch the whisky-ed cloth to her gash. The only way she implied she was in pain was by breathing out sharply and clenching her hands.

"You have quite the steel nerves, Ms. DeLaney. Many men have cried out with this whisky to a mere paper cut."

She smiled. "Call me Charlotte, please. And you are...?"

"Erique. I am only Erique."

"All right, only Erique." She paused for a moment. "Your hands are surprisingly warm."

"I beg your pardon?"

"Your hands are quite warm. I thought you'd be cold, considering your pale complexion."

"Not all that is pale is cold, Charlotte."

"Yes, that was quite presumptuous of me. After all, the night can be warm."

"It can be, if one has someone to share those hours with."

"Do you not, Erique?"

He scoffed. "Of course not. I assume you have suitors."

"None that suit me."

He raised his eyebrows. "Really?"

"The world of dimwitted dandies and aristocratic fools is not one I wish to belong to." She rolled her eyes. "I prefer intelligence and art over money. Those who try to talk about art, who speak of what they don't know—they come off as trite, do they not? For example, I ran into a man, his last name was Gray, a few weeks ago in Paris." She pursed her lips tightly in agitation for a brief moment. "He was so pompous with how he talked, how he dressed. He said to me he had never been with one who had a 'voice of an angel'. I told him I would not be with a man who had the needs of a devil."

Erik sighed. It was times like this, that he felt thankful that he didn't fit in with most of society. "Did such a man honestly believe that a woman of your caliber would simply...?" He shook his head. "What an uncivilized cur. Those such as him hide their beastliness behind wealth and stature. I find it is the only way they can hide. As for myself—I have nothing to hide behind."

She touched her fingertips to his hand that was poised over her shoulder. "I am glad, Erique. I like what I see."

He swallowed, turning away so he could rinse the washcloth in the basin. He was thankful for the distraction. He had to calm the heat rising within him. She looked at a shelf of books at the foot of the cot, and reached over to run her hands along the spines of the tomes.

"Where did you find all these books, Sir Erique?" She asked.

"I am no knight, Charlotte."

She smiled. "Well, I have been a queen time and time again on stage," she chirped, playfully. "So thus, I have the power to knight you. From now on, you will be Sir Erique of the Under Stage."

He moved back toward her with the newly wetted cloth and dabbed it delicately on the wound to cool the alcoholic sting. "In my travels, fair one. In my travels."

"Where have you been?"

"Before coming here, I found myself in Germany, Russia, Spain, Ireland, and Vienna. The cover of night gives me the freedom to roam."

"Is language not a barrier?"

"Do you assume I do not know the language?"

"I assumed you erudite; however well-traveled and spoken is not something I would guess. I thought with the challenges you face...."

"Der Schein kann täuschen, Fräulein."

The right corner of her mouth lifted. "German. Your accent is quite good." She shifted her shoulder uncomfortably. "I apologize, it still stings."

He set the washcloth aside and gently blew on the freshly cleaned wound, cooling it. To his surprise, she leaned back against him, her spine hitting his chest.

"You're colder here," she said. "Why is that?"

"I have circulation issues. You probably thought my hands were warm because of the gaslights. Does my temperature bother you?"

"No."

"Still, I apologize."

"Why? I just said no. The stage lights can be so warm—I sometimes appreciate the cold." She settled into him. "I saw a few poetry collections on your shelf. Who is your favorite poet?"

"Other than Shakespeare?

"Everyone says Shakespeare. *I* say Shakespeare. Pick someone else."

"John Clare. I love his work."

"As do I! I adore him. You're the first person who has said that."

"Is he your favorite as well?"

"Close, but I like Alfred Noyes."

"The Highway Man!"

"Yes, you know it?"

He cleared his throat:

"One kiss, my bonny sweetheart, I'm after a prize to-night
But I shall be back with the yellow gold before the morning light;
Yet, if they press me sharply, and harry me through the day,
Then look for me by moonlight
Watch for me by moonlight,
I'll come to thee by moonlight, though hell should bar the way."

"You could be an actor, Sir Erique," she said breathlessly.

He motioned to his face. "Not in this lifetime."

"Then, I will be your audience of one. Do you have any Clare memorized?"

"Yes," he said, turning his cheek to touch her forehead. "If you command it:

I am—yet what I am none cares or knows;
My friends forsake me like a memory lost:
I am the self-consumer of my woes—
They rise and vanish in oblivious host,
Like shadows in love's frenzied stifled throes
And yet I am, and live—like vapours tossed
Into the nothingness of scorn and noise,
Into the living sea of waking dreams,
Where there is neither sense of life or joys,
But the vast shipwreck of my life's esteems;
Even the dearest that I loved the best
Are strange—nay, rather, stranger than the rest.
I long for scenes where man hath never trod
A place where woman never smiled or wept
There to abide with my Creator, God,
And sleep as I in childhood sweetly slept,
Untroubling and untroubled where I lie
The grass below—above the vaulted sky."

She hummed quietly in delight, her head falling back onto his shoulder. "Sir Erique, you are a knight of poetry. You will defend the written word, so I command it."

"My mistress of music, as long as you sing my soul, I am yours to control."

"Is that Clare?"

"No," he whispered. "That's my own creation."

There was a comfortable silence between them, before her delicate voice shot through the air.

"You were cleaning my wound," she teased. "You became distracted."

He realized then he had wrapped one arm around her waist, the other across her upper chest with his right hand gripping her uninjured shoulder. He was unknowingly pulling her to him, his lips so close he could kiss the tip of her ear.

"I'm sorry," he said, slipping his arms away. "I will..."

She gripped his forearm to stop him. "The wound can wait."

"My lady, it really mustn't." But he made no move to pull away.

She adjusted herself subtly so she was sitting in between his legs. Her fingers moved to entwine with his, her lower back close to his...

"Forgive me," he said suddenly, forcing himself from her. "I have crossed boundaries with you. None of this is proper, and I had no right to take advantage. Please, let me finish attending to you, and then you must fly from here. Remember me in soft gaslight whispering poetry for you. That is all I can ask for."

"Erique, please!" She stood with him. "I—I'm not like this. I am not a woman who throws herself at strangers. I have had one or two close relationships of the physical nature, but none—none have spoken to the heartbeat of me like you have. Believe me, when you took me down here, I was not expecting such a thing to occur. But this place with you has become a secret haven."

"You're young, you don't..."

She held up a hand, stopping him mid-sentence. "Do not mistake me for some simpering English woman who lived her rich life off of crumpets and tea! I was in this place before you were. I saw horrors created here and in my own life. I fear nothing. I don't fear scars. I don't fear heartbreak. I only fear that I will leave your domain and never completely..." Her voice trailed off.

"What, my sweet dear?"

She raised her eyes to him. "Never know *you*." She took a step toward him, her hand reaching out to run over the buttons of his coat. "Highwayman, your Bess awaits."

He backed away from her. "I can't. You don't understand, Charlotte. I don't—I don't know how to do this."

"Your hands have done what mine have. You created on this stage." She leaned in and whispered, "Create with me, if you want to. Just tell me if you don't want to."

His shaking hands took hers. "I do. I just don't know how."

"I'm not afraid. Let me guide you?"

He nodded. "Yes."

She made the first move. She freed her right hand and brought it to the back of his head, pushing his lips forward to meet hers in a gentle kiss.

He gave in to her, wrapping his hands around her waist, feeling through her shirt that she was wearing a corset. His tongue met hers in a passionate dance, and she began to unbutton his jacket. He realized her actions then and grabbed her wrists.

"No, stop...please." His voice trembled. "I don't want you to see my scars. What is underneath is worse than my face. I know my visage is merely tolerable, but below...I don't want my last memory of you to be you running from me, screaming."

Her brow furrowed in concern. "Do you worry so much?"

He nodded. "Yes."

She looked at him compassionately. "I understand, Erique. Here." She ripped the rest of the sleeve away from her shirt and handed the strip to him. "Blindfold me then."

His eyebrows rose. "Do you trust me so?"

"You've already touched me using poetry. In a way, we've been intimate...this is just a step."

"It means more to me than that, sweet woman."

With a kiss and smile, she handed the blindfold over to him. "Just promise me something."

"Yes?"

"I—I don't want to have a child. I do worry about such things."

"I will be careful with you." He kissed her forehead gently. "Nothing like that will come from our union."

She nodded and bowed her head. He tied the blindfold around her eyes, securing it tightly in the back. After, his hand trailed down her cheeks and lifted her face for another deep kiss. Her arms wrapped around his neck, as her lower body pressed into his aroused state. A gasp escaped him, and instinctually, his grip on her tightened. He lowered her carefully onto the cot, his mouth leaving wet, teasing kisses on her neck as he did so.

"I will honor you with my touch," he whispered into her ear. "I swear it." He kissed her temple and smoothed back her hair. "If I cause distress and discomfort to you, please tell me. I never..." He took a deep breath. "I would never want to hurt you."

Charlotte reached for his hand, bringing his knuckles to her lips. "Never has anyone else had such concern for my body. I wish you could look into my eyes and see how it moves me."

His mouth hovered above hers. "I will look upon you when you have an afterglow."

He lifted his fingertips to her shoulders and then moved them lower to the curve of her breasts. Her gentle smile and soft sighs gave him permission to continue. His hips moved against hers as he explored and touched her. Moments later, he began unbuttoning her shirt, fumbling with the buttons in his excitement.

"Erique, talk to me," she requested. "Please? The silence can be daunting."

"I apologize, my lady. What do you wish for me to say?"

"Whatever is on your heart."

He took a deep breath. "Ah, yes, I know."

As he was pushing the shirt off her shoulders he began his recitation.

"Come to my heart, you tiger I adore
You sullen monster, cruel and speechless spirit;
Into the thickness of your heavy mane
I want to plunge my trembling fingers' grip."

He tossed the shirt away, her top clad in only a silken white corset. He moved his lips over the edge of the bosom, allowing them to brush against the skin as he continued speaking.

"I want to hide the throbbing of my head
In your perfume, under those petticoats,
And breathe the musty scent of our old love,
The fading fragrance of the dying rose."

He rolled his hips into hers, like he heard other lovers do. His hands held her waist fast so she couldn't roll against him. It was so tantalizing—he could see in her strained face her struggle to keep control. He backed his hips away and gently pressed his palm upon her most sacred place. She cried out, pushing into his touch. With his free hand he expertly began to free her from the corset.

"I want to sleep! to sleep and not to live!
And in sleep as sweet as death, to dream
Of spreading out my kisses without shame
On your smooth body, bright with copper sheen."

He finally had to use both hands to undo the hook and eye clasps, and at the sight of her chest, stopped short. He had read anatomy books. He knew what women looked like. But still, seeing it all in reality—no words nor illustrations could capture the experience of seeing a woman he cared for, exposed. He at first didn't notice that, where her nipples should be, there were brown, swirled scars.

When the realization hit him, he said nothing. He gingerly touched the marks allowing silence to ask the questions for him.

"You are not the only one with scars," she said.

He looked up at her blindfolded face. "You're beautiful. Were—were you born like this?"

"No. When I was a child I leaned over a candle and my dress caught fire. Most of the scars have faded. The missing of tits hasn't. It is one of the reasons I don't want children."

"Words to describe you escape me. Your scars don't repel me, no, in fact they do quite the opposite." He leaned over her right breast, his breath covering it. "Oh, blessed be, my Charlotte."

His lips closed over the scar, his tongue flicking it experimentally. Her body jumped in response, but she welcomed it. His left hand reached up to her untouched breast and began to massage it gently. He teasingly scraped his teeth against her flared areolas, his body once more moving against her. While he worshipped her chest she began to unbutton his great coat, and as he was consumed with her, he failed to notice until she tried to pull it off of him. He backed away from her to remove the garment, and soon he was lying upon her once more.

"Erique," she whimpered. "Erique..."

He grinned, moving his mouth from her chest to her lips. His fingers buried themselves in her hair, and he didn't stop until he felt her palm press firmly to his chest.

He backed away from her. "Was I being too forceful?"

She smiled. "No, you were excellent. In fact, I thought you were being quite gentle."

"Then what troubles you? Do you want me to stop? I will if you command it. This was enough, worry not about..."

"No, I don't want to stop, unless you do."

"No, no! I don't want to take advantage."

"You haven't." She began to finger the buttons of his dark coveralls. "I want you naked with me, please?"

He looked down, thankful she could not see the anxiety upon his face. "Yes, of course. That is why you're blindfolded." He stood from her to disrobe. "If you feel me, and are frightened, we can stop." With shaking fingers, he began to unbutton his coveralls, and after they were stripped to his waist, he took off his shirt. He looked at his scarred body, self-loathing filling him. To push him through the moment, he began to recite more poetry.

"If I would swallow down my softened sobs
It must be in your bed's profound abyss-
Forgetfulness is moistening your breath,
Lethe itself runs smoothly in your kiss."

He slid the coverall bottoms off, and afterwards his underclothing as well.

"My destiny, from now on my delight,
Is to obey as one who has been sent
To guiltless martyrdom, when all the while
His passion fans the flames of his torment."

He approached the bed, lying not above but beside her. He pulled her close to him, kissing her face, hoping his nakedness would not cause her stress. In between kisses he finished the stanza.

"My lips will suck the cure for bitterness:
Oblivion, nepenthe has its start
In the bewitching teats of those hard breasts,
That never have been harbour of the heart."

She sighed audibly as her hands roamed over his chest and shoulders. Either she could not feel his raised scars or she chose to not mention them, for she didn't say a word. It was even possible that she was a good enough woman that they didn't matter.

"You have a strong body," she said.

"Thank you."

"No, thank you for the poetry. That was—that was almost spiritual." She moved her palm down his stomach and then to his aroused member. He didn't know what women preferred, but by the way she began stroking him, he was able to conclude she liked his length.

After a few moments, his hands unbuttoned the pants she wore, and he slid them down her legs. His mouth fell open in surprise. She was not wearing any undergarments.

"They aren't very comfortable," she said, guessing his thoughts.

Her body was exquisite. Her curves were firm, but supple. Her thighs looked powerful, as did her calves before sloping into dainty ankles and feet. His hands roamed up and down her legs, and gazing at her sacred womanhood...he wondered.

He bent over her, his breath at her folds. He kissed her open chasm a few times before dipping his tongue inside. She gasped in pleasure and raised her body to his mouth. He tried to recollect what he read in the *Kama Sutra*, thankful that he picked it up out of sheer curiosity. He gently rolled his tongue inside of her, exploring her crevices, until the tip of his tongue touched a very sensitive nub.

"Erique," she uttered. "Oh Christ...Erique..."

He licked that precious spot over and over, teasing it with his tongue before simply lapping at it. She squirmed beneath him, but the tight grip her fingers held to the back of his head told him to continue his work. He did so, tirelessly, until...

She screamed, her body shaking beneath him. He knew, from medical textbooks, that she was orgasming. He remembered from novels and personal diaries that it was difficult for a man to get a woman to that state. He couldn't help but feel slight pride.

He took his mouth away from her, wiping away their communion with the back of his hand. He gathered her in his arms, pulling her body close to his.

"We can stop," he said. "You just did a very remarkable thing, my..."

"I don't want to stop," she said, breathlessly laughing. "That was incredible, Erique!"

He smiled. "Was it?"

"Yes, my love, yes."

He started. "Love?"

She reached for him, pulling his head to her chest. "I know what I said," she whispered.

"I don't deserve it."

"I will say what feelings of mine you do or don't deserve." She kissed the top of his head. "Erique...I want you inside me."

He backed away to look at her. "Are you certain?"

"Yes. I am very, very certain."

He kissed her, his lips merely touching hers. "Let us begin, my songstress."

He gently settled his weight above her, his member against her entrance. She was still wet; this was something he was thankful for. It would make their lovemaking easier. Perhaps him entering her would not be uncomfortable. He carefully positioned himself, his tip poised at her beginning.

"We can always stop, no matter where we are in this," he reassured. He took a deep breath. "Do you want me to enter quickly, or slowly?"

"Quickly, I think. I feel like I'm on fire, Erique, and only you can tame it."

"Then hold onto me, Charlotte."

He pushed himself inside of her to the hilt. She let out a cry as his eyes widened. He didn't expect her to be so tight around him. He didn't expect it to feel so incredibly warm and wet. He could feel himself pulsing against her walls, and he gave himself a few moments to become accustomed to how she felt.

He pumped himself inside of her, only able to utter her name repeatedly. "Charlotte, oh Christ, Charlotte…"

He felt her fingernails on his back, the pain only making their communion more intense. He breathed in deeply, burying his face in her soft locks. She smelled of sandalwood and honey. He closed his eyes, trying to experience her momentary world of darkness with the blindfold. Touch, smell, and hearing became heightened. He could hear the gentle hitch in her breathing whenever he pushed himself into her. He could feel her small movements below him as she tried to become even closer to his body, if such a thing were possible. His hand moved across her back, and under his palm, he could feel her shoulders rise and fall as her lungs deflated and once more filled. He realized, unconsciously, his breathing matched hers. He wondered if his heartbeat did…

His palm covered her upper chest, that sloping space between shoulder and round bosom. Her heart was slower than his by three seconds. He took a deep breath, and focused on the darkness behind his eyelids. He swore, by sheer will, he stilled his heart to catch up with hers.

His eyes fluttered open, and gazing at her, he realized she seemed more radiant than ever. He touched the back of his hand to her cheek, and she reached up to catch his fingers. She brought the tips of them to her lips and kissed them in a flurry. Even though they were doing the most adulterous thing he could imagine, she looked so innocent and sweet in that moment.

"May I try touching you?" He asked sheepishly.

"In what way, my knight?"

"I want to feel us connected."

She kissed him softly. "You do not need permission to do that. You may touch me anywhere you like. I mean that."

He withdrew his hand from hers and trailed his fingertips down her body. She giggled at the ticklish touch, which made him smile. He rarely smiled, but this remarkable woman gave him heights of joy he had never known.

Finally, he felt her folds, right where his member met her entrance. He gasped, such a thing so surreal. Two humans connected in this way, fitting so perfectly—such a thing only came from love stories or other scandalous texts. His fingers searched for that sensitive nub once more, and when she moaned at his touch, he began his ministrations.

"You're relentless," she moaned.

"I want you happy." He leaned in, his tongue circling around her ear. "Is such a thing too much to ask?"

"I am able to give you my happiness easily." She gasped as his fingertips circled her clit. "Erique, I'm going to come again."

"You say it shamefully."

"Some say it is a shame for a woman to enjoy this."

He quickened his movements. "They are wrong."

Before the dry sobbed ripped out of her, he could tell she was coming by the tightening around his cock. The cry followed. He moved faster in her to prolong her orgasm, pushing against her almost violently. She collapsed beneath him, her arms sliding from his back.

"Did you come yet?" She asked, a smile on her face.

"No, my sweet. I have not. Do we need to stop? Have I worn you?"

"No. I want you—*this*—for as long as I can have it."

"Well, here. Rest with me for a second. I won't withdraw." He wrapped his arms around her waist and turned, so they were both on their sides, but he was still inside her. He reached up to massage her shoulders and loosen the tension he had built up in her.

"I want to see you," she stated.

He froze. "What?"

"I want to see you, Erique. I want to see our bodies connected."

"Charlotte, I must beseech you—I cannot allow you to see me as a monster. My body is a patchwork doll at best."

"How could I detest the body and mind that takes me to new heights?"

"Fear and hatred is something I know well. Charlotte, if the world knew the acts you were doing with me right now your career would be ruined." He kissed the corner of her mouth. "How could I curse you to live in scorn and mockery?"

She paused. "You could marry me. You could take my name. It would protect you."

He took a deep breath. "No. You're so young. You don't know...you don't know the ways of this Earth."

"I know many who have married for less. I know others who have done more reckless things."

"I understand you grew up poor, among the wretched like me. But I think you have been removed far too long to understand."

"You underestimate me!"

"No! You are an angel, and if you knew you were making love to a demon—"

"I am making love to the night!"

He placed a finger on her lips. "Your idealism moves me to tears, my Charlotte."

"If you dare to call me yours, then take my name."

"I do not dare to end your life and career."

"Then let me see you. Let me gaze upon you and I will make that decision."

He took a deep breath and brought his hands to the back of her head, his fingers on the knot of the blindfold. "I—I cannot deny you. Charlotte, I could have loved you in another life." For a moment, he dared to dream. In the safety of her darkness and acceptance—he fantasized for a moment. "We might have had a good union. I would have been a good husband." He untied the blindfold, tears in his eyes.

"When I waked..." he whispered, watching her eyes flutter open. *"I cried to dream again."*

When her eyes adjusted to the light and focused on his face, she smiled gently. But then they lowered to his chest where his patchwork scars were more prominent.

The composure from earlier slipped. Her hand flew to cover her mouth, her eyes gathered with tears. Fear flashed across her face and from behind her palm, he heard a muffled cry. Her hands began to shake as her fingers traced the scars. Her whole body began to shiver, and he started to back away from her.

"I'm sorry," he said, his voice strained. "I'm so, so sorry. Forget you saw me. You owe me nothing, nothing..."

"NO!" She gripped his shoulders and pulled him back. "No, Erique—I only cry for you out of pity. It's shocking, but I have been with pretty men, and no man has been able to cradle my mind like you have. I take your mind and your scars above all other men any day."

His hands clenched as his breathing hitched. "You are making love with a corpse."

"I am making love with a man I care for." She hooked her leg behind his knee and pulled him to her again. He gasped at their sudden closeness and, like he was moving a few minutes ago trying to become one with her, it was now her body moving closer to his. He gasped at her rolling hips, her breasts that aligned with his chest with every thrust.

And then tears wet his eyes and ran down his cheeks before he could stop them. She kissed the tracks, as though trying to erase his pain with each touch. He did not want her pity; he only wanted her to bear witness to the emotions inside of him, the storm that he could not name. He pressed his mouth to hers, daringly biting her bottom lip. She groaned, and with that he spun downward into his passion again.

"Charlotte, Charlotte, Charlotte..." He wrapped his arms around her waist in an ironclad grip. "Do you trust me?"

She nodded. "Yes. My body is yours."

He rolled so she was on top of him, her upper body lying on his chest, and he bucked his hips into hers.

"Keep your legs tight to my sides. You need to hold onto me." Her arms slid around his neck. "That's a good girl." He kissed the side of her face.

He felt a power inside of him he had never before as he stood from the bed and carried her to the opposite wall. He pinned her there, her back hitting a wooden beam. He kissed her ravenously, feeling the beam vibrate with every thrust.

"Your eyes," she whispered with a smile, "your eyes are pure emerald. I thought they were dark, but you shine. Do you know you shine, Erique?" She kissed the scars on the side of his face.

"You do," he breathed into her mouth as he caught her lips for a kiss. "I heard you shine in a wax cylinder. You fought against my loneliness, but did not know it. And now you trust me...to hold, to adore."

"You now have my body."

"We have each other's bodies."

She clenched around him at his words, and he felt she could use more...auditory stimulation. He sighed.

"When, with both my eyes closed, on a hot autumn night,
I inhale the fragrance of your warm breast
I see happy shores spread out before me,
On which shines a dazzling and monotonous sun..."

She smiled into his neck as his thrusts almost kept time with the poem.

"A lazy isle to which nature has given
Singular trees, savory fruits,
Men with bodies vigorous and slender,
And women in whose eyes shines a startling candor."

"Erique, please..."

He kissed her forehead. "I like that. Yes. You make my name sound so gentle and soft. *Guided by your fragrance to these charming countries,*

I see a port filled with sails and rigging

Still utterly wearied by the waves of the sea..."

"I'm close."

"I know." He quickened his thrusts. *"While the perfume of the green tamarinds,*

That permeates the air, and elates my nostrils,

Is mingled in my soul with the sailors' chanteys..."

"Yes! Yes!"

This time she did not cry; her voice only coming out as a hoarse whisper. He had worn her. Her reaction was not as dramatic, but still he felt that squeezing once more around him.

"You are tired. Let us dress, and I will make sure you are safely returned to your abode."

"No. you haven't come yet."

He touched his forehead to hers. "I don't know if I can."

"Is—is there something wrong with me?"

"No, of course not. I—I dare not say it."

"Say it."

"Such a thing is crude."

"We have just done the crudest thing I can think of. Tell me."

He whispered it, like a confession, in her ear. "I may have to fuck you."

She looked at him daringly. "Then fuck me."

"I cannot promise gentleness."

"I said, fuck me."

He carried her back to the bed and, with a smile, pinned her arms above her head. He buried his face in her neck as he thrust himself into her with abandon. She gasped as his teeth scraped against her skin, his thrusts becoming rougher. She whimpered and he stilled.

"We can stop," he said.

"Fuck me."

"As you wish."

He continued his work, her legs wrapping themselves around his waist. He lost track of time as he continued to worship her body in his own, rough way. He felt a sensation, something that called for his continuing sheathing inside her. Her body lifted to meet his actions; her moaning encouraged him. He was close, he—he was—

"By the heavens!"

He quickly retreated from her, spilling his seed onto the sheets. He felt something rip through him, pushing him to eternity. He closed his eyes as the sensation met its peak. And then—it stopped, he felt his body withering, and a calm spread from his stomach to the ends of his limbs.

He collapsed upon her, his head lying on her shoulder. She too was breathing heavily, but still she reached up to smooth his hair back and kiss his cheek.

"It's all right," she said. "I'm here. Worry not. I'm here..."

He didn't have a voice to describe what had just occurred. He seemed to lose all sense of any languages he had learned. He looked to her, asking for description. He only received the vision of tears in her eyes, a smile upon her face.

Not knowing what else to do or how to describe the happiness inside of him, he buried his face in her shoulder, and recited poetry to her in the dark.

Part Two:

The Stories Scars Tell

*

Erique did not need sleep. Instead, he tidied his hovel under the stage while Charlotte DeLaney slumbered. He even carefully dressed her wound while her world of dreams kept her from feeling pain. He dressed quietly when his pocket watch struck six in the morning. Even knowing she accepted him; he did not want her seeing his scarred body when she first awoke.

To pass the time he read quietly, and around eight o'clock, she stirred. He was sitting on the floor, his back up against the wall, positioned so he could keep an eye on her. He observed that she automatically reached for his side of the cot, her hands beginning to search for something. Seconds later it occurred that she was reaching for him.

"Good morning," he said.

She turned to him, the covers pooling at her waist to reveal she was in one of his shirts. He had slipped it over her while she rested. She touched the collar of it, smiling.

"Thank you," she sighed. "Good morning, Sir Erique. Why are you not in bed with me?" Her face fell. "Have I fallen out of your favor so quickly?"

He pushed himself up from his sitting position and walked over to her swiftly. "No, Charlotte. I—I didn't want to intrude or startle you." He sat beside her on the edge of the bed.

She raised a hand to touch his cheek. "The only thing that shocked my system was that you were not beside me when I reawakened."

"Forgive me, and I will remedy that."

He laid down beside her, pulling her close to his chest. Her arms wrapped around him and he felt that familiar heat rising within him once more. He was brave, softly kissing her mouth before diving in deeper. He forgot that there was rehearsal. He forgot that the cast would arrive in two hours. For a moment they were the only two in their private universe.

She backed away to pull his shirt over her head. She reached for his overall buttons, and instinctively, he crossed his arm over them. Charlotte, with the patience of a teacher, stretched over and gripped his forearm.

"My mind hasn't changed since last night. Sir Erique, claim your queen."

He shook his head. "I am not a knight, my lady. We cannot pretend I am. I am the dragon."

"Nothing changes. Claim the queen, dragon."

He lowered his arm and finally she was granted access to his buttons. She undid them, lowering the upper portion of his overalls, to take his shirt off. When it joined her temporary night shirt on the ground, she then removed his bottoms. When he was naked with her once more, she studied his body.

"I didn't get to do this last night," she whispered. "You kept me in darkness."

"I was afraid."

"And are you now?"

His eyes met hers and he shook his head. "No. I think not."

He pulled her to his chest roughly, and her fingers traced his scars once more. "What happened to you, Erique?"

"It was a factory accident. I already had health problems before and...."

"No. These are surgical scars. What *happened* to you?"

His eyes darted to her face, his stomach feeling like someone dropped a sack of bricks on it. "How did you know?"

"When I was working here, the costume mistress and I would go to hospitals and visit patients. Concerning makeup and clothing, we wanted to make sure what we were doing here was accurate. When I left the theater and was given proper training in Paris, I had access to libraries and I sought out medical textbooks. Your face could be construed as accidental scarring, but the scars on your chest are surgical, leading me to think what is on your face is so as well. You—you even..."

He hung his head. "Say it, Charlotte. I know you will."

She breathed out slowly. "It looks like an autopsy has been performed on you. Please, Erique—were you in an asylum somewhere? Did—-something medically...?" Her voice trailed off. "I—I don't care; such things don't matter to me. I only want honesty between us and I want to know you, even the darker things."

"My origins are darker than nightmares." He reached forward on the mattress and took her hand. "I don't want your view of me to be tainted. For me, this is enough. Last night—was enough."

"But there is more, Erique. There can be more."

"No, not for me. Our union would be a damned one, a cursed one."

"Tell me your story. Let me be the judge of that."

"I've suffered enough in my life. I cannot—to lose you..."

"You won't lose me." She threw her arms around him. "Why don't you trust me?"

"I do, Charlotte." He smoothed her hair back, resting his chin on top of her head as he did. "I think I am beginning to love you, as naive and careless as that is. I cannot deny you anything."

"And I grant you my love. Now bless me with your trust."

He held her with shaking arms, tears threatening to burst forth once more. Damn, damn. He wasn't one to cry and here she was, cutting him to the quick emotionally.

"Kiss me," he begged. "Please...I want one more sweet memory before I lose you."

"You won't lose me, but if it comforts you, I offer you myself."

"No, Charlotte, I want *you* to kiss *me*."

She looked up at him. "Of course, my darling."

She pulled her face level with his and their lips touched. Her hands buried themselves in his hair, and as they backed away, he took a ragged breath.

"Charlotte," he wept, "forgive me for what I am about to say..."

*

He held her as she retched into the basin. She still clung to him; somehow, she could still stand to touch him. She cried as her insides emptied. His tears had since dried. When he saw the look of horror on her face; he knew his time for vulnerability was gone.

When Charlotte was finished, he gently sat her back on the cot. Without saying a word he pulled on his coveralls, grabbed the basin, and walked upstairs to empty it.

Her reaction wasn't unexpected. How could one understand that his father used him for medical experiments? How could one process calmly that Erique, at the age of eight, ran away from his home because he was tired of being cut open, tired of almost dying from infections every few weeks? He hadn't known when he left that such surgical scars cursed him to live the life of a pariah in society. However, it was better than the world of blood, muscle, and knives he had left behind.

He filled the basin with fresh water in the lavatory and made his way back to his domain. Erique saw that she had laid down on the cot, her body shivering. Grabbing a cup from one of the shelves, he poured some water for her.

Wordlessly, he held it out to her, keeping his gaze away.

"I'm sorry," he said softly. "I'm sorry."

"Oh Erique," she uttered. "Oh dear, dear Erique."

She took the cup, their hands brushing. His heart leapt to his chest.

"This does complicate things," she said.

"Yes. Yes, it does." His shoulders rose. "I told you; you fucked a corpse—an experiment."

"Do you hate me for my questions?"

"No. I hate myself."

"I apologize for my reaction. I was not prepared."

"I was."

"Stop. What I did was inexcusable. You are no monster." She sighed deeply. "I'm sorry for what you went through. I'm sorry the first years of childhood were filled with pain. I wish I had been there, to hold you. To care for you!"

"You cannot look upon me without fear, now knowing what you know."

She sat up and ripped the buttons from his coveralls, the top falling from him. She gazed at him, placing her hands gently on his pectorals—over one of his scars that crisscrossed, making an X over his heart.

"Do not tell me what my limitations are. I love you, Erique."

He was not gentle as he pulled her to him and crushed his lips to hers. She reached around his back to pull his coveralls down. He was naked with her once more, and she rolled over so she was above him. She moved herself into a sitting position, her body resting, hovering above his member. They looked at each other briefly before she reached down and guided him inside of her. He gasped and closed his eyes.

She moved up and down, the cot bouncing with her weight. He placed his hands at her hips to help guide and steady her. Out of the corner of her eye, she saw her blindfold in the sheets. She reached for it, grabbed his hands, and tied his wrists together. She pinned them above his head, stooping down for a moment to bestow kisses on his face.

She swirled her body around him and he bucked his hips into hers. She let out a cry, stopping her previous movements to meet his upward thrusts.

"Touch yourself," he breathed.

"What?"

He opened his eyes, his blue irises piercing through her. "Touch yourself, like I touched you."

She laughed softly. "I shall."

Her fingers touched that delicate bud, circling it with her finger like he had. Focusing on herself she began to slow her bobbing rhythm above him. He took over, powerfully thrusting upward so her internal and external sensation matched.

Her moans became louder, her back arching. "Erique!"

He felt her orgasm squeezing him and her shoulders shook. She made no noise; her head only inclined upward, a quiet smile upon her face as though she were basking in her body's accomplishment. He moved to sit up, her legs wrapping themselves around his sides. He took her face in his bound hands and kissed her.

She slipped his arms overhead so they could wrap around her neck. They began to move together, chest to chest, gazing at one another during their lovemaking. He moved forward to kiss her deeply, his tongue beginning to match the rhythm of his thrusts.

"Can we try something?" She asked.

"What do you wish for, my lady?"

"Take me from behind."

He gave a mischievous smile. "*My lady.*"

"No, I mean...not from my posterior, but..."

"I know, I know." He pulled out of her and gave her space to get on all fours. He moved behind her, angling himself at her entrance. "If this hurts, let me know."

"I will."

He gripped her hips as he entered her, the unexpected tightness making his eyes widen. "My God, Charlotte! My Shakespearian heroine, my—my..."

"Yes Erique?" She gasped.

"My whore of the dark."

"Drop your eloquence. I don't think it has a place here."

He pulled her up with him so they were both simply on their knees. He grabbed her breasts roughly to keep her back against his chest, and his lips circled her ear.

"You do not wish for eloquence?" He whispered. "Fine. I can give you roughness. I can show you my power. I want to fuck you. I want to fuck you until you cannot walk. I want to empty my seed into your greedy entrance until I am spent. You are my lover, my paramour, my slut. You are mine and mine alone, do you understand?"

"Oh God, yes."

He kissed her shoulder. "That's my good girl." And then he bit down.

She cried out at the unexpected pleasure. It hurt, but he did not break her skin. There would only be a bruise, and she found the pain heightened all she was feeling. "You can keep talking like this," she sighed.

"You are greedy," he said. "Your quim tightens around me, almost pulls my member into your body. You just want to milk me, don't you? You are too selfish. You are wild. Do I need to tame you?"

"No, no, master."

He gripped her hair and pulled it back. "Yes, I am your master." He began to pound into her harder, his breathing becoming ragged. "Do you want to come, my good girl?"

"You view me as so young?"

"When you have lived through all I have, everyone around you is young. Now, answer me."

"Yes. I want to come."

He paused. "I may not let you, my dear little slut. I may just have my way with you, and then make you touch yourself when I am done." He turned to her ear. "I may have you touch yourself with my seed."

"You are cruel to me," she said, giggling slightly.

"Take my 'cruelty' then. I will give you nothing else." He pushed her onto all fours again, pulling his bound wrists around her neck and in front of her face. "Free me from these. I have work to attend to."

She reached up, steadying herself on her elbows, and freed his wrists. With one hand he grasped her hair and pulled, and with the other he reached down and began to rub her clit.

"I've decided to take care of you," he whispered. "I am being quite rough with you, after all." He paused for a moment, his hands stilling. "Is this fine, Charlotte? I am not hurting you, am I?"

"No, you haven't hurt me. I actually quite enjoy this."

"May I continue?"

"Of course, my dragon."

He rammed into her, his fingers greedily touching her. "Yes, I am your dragon. You asked for this, my queen. I will be the fall of your kingdom. Maybe I will push my seed inside you, and you will bear my children. Our reign will be one of animal and human."

"I do not see you as an animal."

"It doesn't matter how you see me. It is what I am."

His hand left her hair and he ran his nails down her back. "Harder," she begged.

He obliged, leaving smarting, red marks on her shoulder blades. She pushed her lower body into him, as though trying to cool her fresh markings against his chilled skin. He raked his nails down her thighs, over and over again, his thrusts becoming ruthless.

He bit the nape of her neck, as he struggled not to come. He wanted to last as long as he could, however—

"We can slow down," he said, gently.

"No, Erique, I like how powerful you are. I like how you have taken control. I don't want to let that go yet."

He withdrew from her quickly, spun her around to face him, and then pushed her back onto the cot.

"I don't want to take you like this," he said, his voice hard. "I want to possess you." He lowered himself on her body and gently slid his cock inside of her. "Yes...this is how I want you."

He pinned her arms above her head, but his movements were not harsh like earlier. He still sheathed himself to the hilt repeatedly and in quick succession, but he was not so intense. Still, just keeping her so helpless to his whim, made his pleasure heighten. He crushed his lips to hers, his tongue finding refuge in her mouth, while their fingers entwined. He pulled back and his hand reached up to take her chin.

"Now I can see my lady's face. My lovely, little whore. Your body ought to be ready for me. Open yourself to me, in all ways earthly." He lowered his mouth to her ear. "Is this all right?"

"Y—yes..."

"Good." He licked her earlobe and settled his forehead on her shoulder, closing his eyes to feel her giving body surrounding him. Goddamn it, he was close. He was right on the edge.

It was two words escaping her plump lips that caused his release.

"Erique, please."

He was gone.

He let out a cry as he withdrew from her, his hand reaching to his member to pump out the rest of his orgasm on her stomach. His climax lasted for a minute at most, but it seemed to go on and on.

He finished at last, his arm shaking. His thighs began to quiver uncontrollably. He was a tireless being, but the past twenty-four hours had taken so much out of him.

"Am I still your whore?" She asked, her voice teasing.

He rolled off of her, taking the sheet and wiping away his seed from her skin. In seconds he was settling himself on his side next to her, and she cuddled close to him. "No. You never are. Even when I play at being your master, you can stop me, and I am back under your control. If anything I did were to truly hurt, I would part from you and beg forgiveness."

"Erique..."

"I know I have hurt you already. Your thighs ache. I was cruel."

"You were excellent. I will savor each moment of that pain knowing the pleasure you gave me. Sometimes, after making so many choices, it is nice to have someone be responsible, to make those choices for me. Today you held this power I did not know the name for. Now," she reached between her legs, "I have to finish what my master ordered me to do."

"I don't recall..." He then gasped. "Oh, yes. I do."

He watched her dip a finger inside of her to retrieve both his and her juices. In a swirling motion she was soon touching herself, her body exerting the last bit of energy it could manage. He pulled her close, gently petting her locks as she pleasured herself. The moment didn't last long. He felt her body delightfully shudder minutes later, and as she rode her climax, he kissed her.

"I love you," he whispered.

Her body went limp in his arms, but he felt her smile into his shoulder. "I love you too, Erique."

*

Charlotte dressed herself in her trousers and torn shirt. Erique laced her corset. There was something intimate in assisting in her dress, even though he didn't know what it was. While she dressed, she sang for him a new aria out of an opera called *Turandot*.

"The Italians love it. We are hoping to bring it to Paris in the summer," she said.

"What is the plot?" Erique asked.

"It's a love story, of course. A man sees the princess, falls in love with said princess, the father doesn't want the man to marry the princess and so on and so forth."

"Ah, of course."

"Yes, we mustn't challenge the regular population with any transcendent thinking," she said sarcastically. "But, the song *is* pretty."

"What is it called?"

"Nessun Dorma."

"Nobody shall sleep."

"Hmhm." She opened her mouth and the lyrics flowed out of her like a river,

"Nessun dorma! Nessun dorma!

Tu pure, o, Principessa,

nella tua fredda stanza,

guardi le stelle

che tremano d'amore

e di speranza."

He smiled as he sat on the cot and watched her sing. She walked about the room, gesturing as though she was on stage.

"Ma il mio mistero è chiuso in me,

il nome mio nessun saprà!

No, no, sulla tua bocca lo dirò

quando la luce splenderà!

Ed il mio bacio scioglierà il silenzio

che ti fa mia!"

She took his hands then, her voice flawlessly rising to her higher register.

"Dilegua, o notte!

Tramontate, stelle!

Tramontate, stelle!

All'alba vincerò!

vincerò, vincerò!"

She then bowed for him, and he pulled his hands away to clap for her.

"Brava, brava! What a gift you have given me!" He helped her from her bow and kissed her. "I find it isn't quite fair, Charlotte. You have come here like a thief in the night and taken my heart. I fear you will leave with it and I will no longer know my own humanity."

"You could have been an actor, Erique. You are quite dramatic at times."

"The situation we are in is a dramatic one. Do you not think so?"

"I find it better than wondering if you'll ever find love. I find it better than living with a passion unrequited."

He nodded. "Who am I to argue with that?"

She grew silent, gripping her hands in his. "I really do want us to keep seeing each other, Erique."

He sighed sadly. "Charlotte..."

"I'm serious."

"We have to look past the fantasy of last night. You barely know me."

"I know enough. If your origin did not frighten me away, then what can?"

"It isn't proper! One must court a young woman and..."

"Who gives a damn about social custom? It's the dawn of a new age. *I* want to court *you*."

"I am a broken man, Charlotte."

"Perfection is boring," she scoffed.

Erique paused, taking her chin in his hand. "How far can we realistically expect to go? I cannot provide for you."

"Yes, because Charlotte DeLaney, darling of the stage, is destitute."

"I can never take you out publicly. As a couple we would never feel the sun upon us."

"The night is beautiful too."

"I would have to be a secret."

"Intrigue is good for the press."

"Charlotte stop!" He placed his hands on her shoulders. "If our relationship were to be known your career would be done. They would take everything away from you!"

"Let them try!"

"They could succeed!"

Tears gathered in her eyes, and his heart melted. "You don't want to be with me," she said quietly.

His face fell. "Charlotte...no..." He pulled her against his chest. "The world won't let me."

"My estate is large. The world is wide."

"But it is not wide enough for us." He kissed the top of her head. "You will find a good man. He will be one of art and chivalry. You two will be married and create your own world, and I will be happy, knowing that meeting me was part of that journey."

"No," she said, sniffling. "No! Fine, we cannot be out in the world and seen. Then we will have our own union on our own terms. I will send for you, when I can. Or I will come here. We will have our moments where we can take them. One day we may have separate partners and separate unions—but we will...we will..."

"We will always find ways to see each other. Always."

Tears fell from her eyes. "This isn't fair!"

"Nothing in my life has been—except for you."

"We have the night." She hugged him tightly. "Let's not waste it."

The Fiddler

Elin Pedersen took a deep breath and checked the tuning of her fiddle one more time. With skill and delicacy, she gripped the neck of the instrument in her right hand and her left lifted the bow, running it across the eight strings of the Hardanger fiddle. She played a few scales, and after a moment or two of tuning, found it on pitch.

She gazed at the instrument, tracing the intricate rosing etched across the body. The artist had been her grandfather, the creator of the fiddle. It was he, a skilled carpenter, who placed the gleaming pearl inlay across the fingerboard, and carved a dragon's head at the top of the tuning pegs. She remembered the story her papa had told her—that her grandfather had made him a violin when they couldn't afford to buy one.

The Pedersens were one of the poorer families who lived near the river, but their abode and living was still a cozy, simple one. Elin's father, Arvid, wasn't a skilled fisher, but he made enough to feed the two of them. They didn't have much in their small, one-room cottage: two single beds for each of them, a chest for belongings, a small wood burning hearth, a table with two chairs, and a desk where she used to work on her studies. In the hearth was a cast iron pot for cooking stews, or the occasional chunk of meat. Jarred vegetables and preservatives sat on a wooden hanging shelf.

But Elin looked at her father's empty bed with a heavy heart. This past winter had been harsher than most. He had been out during the final snow storm of the season, and had caught a cold. It was a simple cough at first, the local doctor had assured. Nothing that warm tea, soup, and bread couldn't fix. But it got worse. And the fever that wouldn't break set in. One night, he encouraged Elin to get some rest, to not worry about him. He was feeling better. She obliged, always one to listen to her loving father. Her father who encouraged her to go to school, who taught her to play the fiddle even though it wasn't "proper".

Elin woke to find Arvid Pedersen gone the next morning. At nineteen she was an orphan. Her father was only forty-eight. He willed her the cottage, and all that belonged inside it, as well as enough money to pay for a pauper's funeral and a few months of food. And, with spring nearing, those funds were running out.

To make them stretch, she performed on the street with her fiddle for coin. Some scoffed but even the skeptics, shocked that a young woman was playing, were still impressed by her skill, throwing her some money here and there. It was enough for thread to fix her clothing, seeds to plant a garden for the upcoming spring, and to keep hunger pains away during the winter. But she wanted more.

Her church was looking for a new fiddler for Sunday mornings and for other weekday performances. Auditions were to take place in five weeks. Others were looking to audition, mainly three men in the area who were highly skilled. More so than her. But she had to try. The weekly pay would be enough to get her a small place in town. Enough to have a comfortable life. She did not want marriage, nor companionship, nor splendor. She just wanted walls where she couldn't hear the winter wind whispering, chilling her and calling her name. Taunting her—that maybe she would meet the same fate as her father.

Her musical talent had to improve, and fast. Elin knew that. She was not naive. And without money to afford lessons, she knew of only one way to possibly make that happen. It wasn't a Chrisitan way, but a folk way that was dying out with the invasion of the Bible. She said the name under her breath: Fossegrimen.

Her father had told her the legend of the river spirit. He claimed it was how he learned to play the fiddle; to go to the river, and give an offering to the mythical being. The elders in Elin's town still whispered this tale to the young children, out of earshot of the church folk of course. They told how Fossegrimen taught their husbands to play, their brothers, their fathers.

Elin was skeptical of these tales, and of such ancient traditions. But, in many ways, honoring the "old ones" had appeared to help her and her father before. Their prayers, their offerings, seemed to give them a better garden and bounty than her neighbors. It was always enough to keep them from starvation, and even at times, give to those who had less. Elin thought it couldn't hurt to try this ritual. It was said, for four Thursdays in a row, one was to give white goat, or the best meat they had, to Fossegrimen. In return, he would teach them the highest skill of the fiddle, an instrument he had mastered throughout his centuries on Earth. But Elin had no meat. She hadn't been able to safely afford some for a long time. But she had another idea.

Elin walked toward her father's trunk, and knelt down to unlatch the clasps. Carefully, she pulled out of the few belongings that remained of her mother's: a red skirt, a starched, high collared white shirt, and a deep green shawl. The skirt was embroidered with delicate white, blue, and orange flowers at the bottom hem. Feeling the shawl in her hands, it felt warm, and thick—perfect for the first few nights of spring, where the winter wind lingered. She carefully put these garments on, and found they fit like a glove. As she wrapped the shawl around her shoulders, she heard something land with a *clink* on the wood floor. Glancing down, she saw it was a simple round, gold locket. Elin picked it up, and pried it open with her fingernail. With a smile, she realized the photographs inside were her mother and father on their wedding day. Sighing, she slipped the chain around her neck.

Sitting in front of the window as a makeshift mirror, she quickly braided her light brown hair. It had a hint of curl, and was best kept in a braid or pulled back in some way. Over that braid and around her head, she tied a handkerchief with green leaves she had sewn into the white fabric. Her eyes, a brilliant blue, shone back at her in the glass. Her pink lips, pursed and anxious, gave a bit of color to her pale face. Freckles danced across the bridge of her nose—freckles she recognized from her papa. The rest of her looks, she had inherited from her mother, something that was confirmed by memory and the locket.

Elin took a deep breath as she grabbed her lace up boots, and slipped them on her feet. She gazed at her fiddle on the table, and put it in the wooden carrying case her grandpa had made. The velvet inside hugged it securely—and Elin wondered if she would ever possess such rich fabric in any other way.

At last, she opened the door to the cottage...and walked to the river bank.

*

It was only a fifteen-minute walk, and the full moon brightly lit Elin's path. It had to be well past ten o'clock, and the few cottages she passed were still. She knew the families inside had to have been sleeping. It wasn't like any of them had a fiddle, or would be attempting such a scheme as hers.

Minutes later, she made it to the river, and carefully climbed down the rocks to its muddy banks. She found a dry, flat rock to set her fiddle case on, and undid the metal latches. She took her time lifting the instrument, noting how beautifully it glistened in the moonlight. Then, she breathed deeply, lifted it under her chin, and began to play. She had no meat to throw into the river—so maybe the mythical Nøkken, the master of music, would be enticed by song.

Soon, she lost herself in her instrument. Something sounded different with her fiddle. The notes seemed to bounce off the rocks, and were enhanced by the wind carrying the sweet sound. Elin always found music an escape from what was around her, but she fell deeper into her playing...

And yet, Fossegrimen didn't magically appear before her. He didn't rise out of the waves, like the old wife's tales spoke. He didn't evaporate out of the air. When Elin lowered the instrument from her shoulder, she chuckled at herself. Of course, this was stupid. This whole thing was foolish. A masculine river spirit, teaching those worthy to play the fiddle, was a wild rumor and mad ravings from old, bored women. Her giggles turned to laughter—-but then her laughter to tears. She fell to her knees, clutching the fiddle to her chest. The loneliness she felt maybe made her delusional. She felt stupid for trying. For hoping. Hope was a thing that didn't belong to girls without fathers, without mothers.

And then, she heard the voice. It was deep, melodic, and—-earthy. Like it could command mountains to bow, wind to cease, even though the voice didn't speak above a whisper.

"You have summoned me," a man said. "You have summoned me...with merely your song."

Elin turned to her right, and her mouth fell. Wearing only tight black pants, dark boots, and shirtless—was a man. He had ruddy, dripping hair like he had just emerged out of the river, yet his clothes weren't wet. His eyes glistened silver, like the moon's reflection on the water. He was a few inches taller than her, and stocky and strong in his build. It made her think of the Vikings—of ancestors long ago.

She quickly stood, and put her violin away.

"It's you...isn't it?" She gasped. "You're...you're Fossegrimen."

He smirked. "No, I am another lunatic river man who is intrigued by song." Elin started at his informal manner, and he laughed. "My dear, after centuries of doing this, I am weary of pleasantries. So, let us just get to it. The meat, please?"

"Wha—what?"

"The meat," he repeated. "The meat that every musician must give, and then after they must play for me and prove they are worthy via skill for me to teach them. You've done things out of order, but since you are decent, I can forgive that."

She sighed. "I—I am the meat," she said.

Fossegrimen's brow furrowed. "What?"

She rolled her shoulders back to let her shawl fall to the ground, and reached up to unbutton the tall collar on her shirt. "I'm poor," she said, quietly, stepping toward him. "So, the meat I offer—is myself. It's—it's my body. I cannot afford meat. Being a musician is my way out of poverty. And if you teach me, for the four Thursdays I come, I will be the offering given."

Something flashed in his eyes, and he swallowed. "Oh—oh by the gods," he whispered.

He walked to her, and Elin saw his eyes flicker up and down her body. He reached up toward her handkerchief around her head. She bit her lip. So, would it really be so unceremonious as this? Would he just take her on the banks there or...

Her thoughts were stopped by him untying the handkerchief, and quickly reaching for her hair. With expert fingers, he untied the long braid, and unwove it. He dug his hands into her scalp, feeling her locks, and loosening them to tumble over her chest. Elin stood stock still, waiting for whatever to come next. But he, for what seemed like eternity, only played with her hair.

And then he backed away.

"Show me how you tune your fiddle," he urged.

She blinked at him. "What?"

"Show me how you tune your fiddle. And then tell me your upkeep of this instrument. Then we will talk about chin placement, and how you are gripping your bow."

"That—that's all you're going to do to me?" She asked.

He smiled, showing white teeth. "Yes. Until next time. Now...show me how you tune your instrument."

*

"Relax your arm a little. You're holding a fiddle, not a gun."

It was the next Thursday, and Elin was once more at the river bank. Fossegrimen was circling her, watching as she held her instrument. So far, this session had been the same as the first. He had watched her respectfully, insisted she let down her hair, but that had been it.

He sighed, listening to her play, and then stepped behind her to adjust her elbow. "Here, you'll find this more suitable..."

Elin was surprised to find his hands warm through the sleeves of her dress. He actually radiated heat, something she didn't expect from a being of the water. She stepped back against him instinctively, her body slightly chilled from the night, seeking warmth.

He started for a moment, and she realized what she had done. Elin breathed deeply.

"I'm sorry," she said, stepping away.

But he wrapped an arm around her waist, and pulled her back to him.

"Keep playing," he softly commanded.

Elin did as he requested, a low-pitched tune that beautifully showed off the darker notes of the fiddle. His splayed hand wandered to the slight swell of her stomach; the music matched his movements. His other palm moved to her skirt, skimming her outer thigh.

"Good," he sighed. "Very good..."

She ignored her own heat, pooling from her chest and lower. She tried to ignore, for a brief moment, the image of his face above her, his hair around her like a curtain.

And as soon as their shared moment happened, he pulled away just as suddenly. Elin turned, and noticed him open and close his hands at his sides, tentatively, as though regretting their emptiness.

"We are done for the night," he said. "Go over the things I critiqued you on."

"Fossegrimen..."

"Until next Thursday."

And in front of her eyes, he walked into the water, and disappeared. She ran to the bank, taking a few steps into the river. The waves came up to her ankles, lapping against them almost hungrily. Elin realized then how fast her heart was beating, how shallow her breath was. She gripped the neck of her violin tightly, and turned back to shore, rushing to place her violin back in its case and hurrying back to her cottage.

*

Elin knew she was improving. With her technical skill being solidified, improvising music became easier. She was able to hear songs from church, and play them by ear on her violin. In preparation for her audition, her day-to-day activities revolved around practicing. She would get up just as the sun peeked over the horizon, make herself a simple breakfast, and then head to town to play in the square for coin. She had noticed that her profits were increasing as well. Not by too much, but it was proof that her lessons with Fossegrimen were fruitful.

She would play for a few hours in the town square, until mid-afternoon. Her day ended with her buying supplies for supper, if needed, and then heading home to eat and rest. She did not perform every day. however.

There were days where she would do simple cleaning around her home and tend the garden, readying it for the upcoming spring. And then, when the sun set, she would get out her violin, and play to the roaring fire in the hearth.

These were the times she cherished the most. In the glow of the flame, she would find herself playing in a way she dared not for anyone else. She danced across the floor, her fiddle singing joyous tunes. Her skirt would swirl around her, rising like waves against a rock. She swayed to the music, tapping out the time signature with her feet.

It was during such an evening session, two days before seeing Fossegrimen, that something—peculiar happened. Elin sat in a chair next to the fire, her skirt lifted to her knees to warm her legs with the flame. She was mopping up her soup bowl with a piece of bread, freshly baked early that morning. When finished, she stood, and placed the bowl on the table, where her violin lay. She picked it up, tucking it under her chin, and ran the bow across the strings.

"Play for me," she heard a deep voice say.

She turned on her heel, looking all about the room for the owner of the voice. Yet the only other sign of movement was the shadows dancing on the wall with the firelight. It hit her then, that the voice sounded like it belonged to Fossegrimen.

"Play for me, please," his voice pleaded.

"Are you here?" She asked.

Only silence responded. But still, she lifted the instrument once more, and played.

Her notes soared through the air, and she began to move to the music once more. As she did so, she felt something pressing against both sides of her waist; feeling like invisible hands.

She jumped, stopping her performance.

"Fosse—F-," she struggled saying the name.

"Call me River when your tongue fails you," he said, his voice not above a whisper.

She took a deep breath, trying to still her shaking body. "Why are you here?"

There was stillness, and suddenly the air felt heavy. Then the response came. "I will leave if you wish. But even a river spirit gets lonely."

Elin sighed, lifting the violin to hold it to her chest. "I understand. Since my father died..."

"I know."

His voice was focused near the hearth, and she turned. There he was, leaning against the wall, his arms crossed.

"I can't hold this form for long," he said. "Not while I am away from the river. But I wanted to hear you." He lowered his arms, and walked toward her. "I am sorry about your father, Elin. I remember his passing;

I know all that goes on in this area. I've known of your family for quite a while."

Her eyebrows rose. "Have you?"

He smiled. "Your grandfather used to sit by my river bank as he crafted the violin you hold. Your family has always had music within. It has just taken until you, to awaken it."

"Is that why you didn't turn me away when we first met?"

"Partially. Elin, please. Play for me."

She studied him, as she lifted her violin under her chin, and placed the bow on the strings. Caught up in the music, she played. The rhythm was fast, celebratory. Her hips moved to the music, her body swaying. Once more, his hands wrapped themselves around her waist, and she looked up to see he was beside her.

She did not stop him, nor protest. His touch was warm, and light against her skin. As she spun to the music, it felt like she was turning in his hands. He stopped her moments later, his palms skimming up her sides, to her shoulder blades, the nape of her neck, and toward her hair. With skilled fingers, he once more loosened her locks from their braid, and untied the kerchief that protected her scalp from the sun. Still, she played, her eyes closing at his touch. A sigh escaped from her lips, and he gently pulled her toward him, her spine hitting his bare chest.

The music stopped, her hand gripping the violin as it dropped to her side. She turned her face toward him; her cheek finding itself upon his skin. It felt like steam was rolling off his exposed chest. Her bow fell with a quiet *clank* to the floor, as she pressed a hand to her heart, to try and still it's beating.

With slight embarrassment, Elin realized she knew the physiological signs of yearning, desire. She could feel her body opening up, readying itself for him. These reactions only happened when she read fictional stories; being transported to places of fantasy where men were chivalrous, noble, and good. The characters in her mind felt safer than men in real life, after all. And when such things occurred, she knew how to fulfill her own desires. To her hands, she was not untouched.

Her head tilted up, her eyes catching his.

"I made you a promise," she whispered.

Fossegrimen put a hand under her chin. "Have you been with another?"

She shook her head. "I've truthfully never been kissed."

"Then no. I would be a monster to ask so much of you in one night." He stepped away, and gently took the fiddle from her hands as he did so. He brought it to his shoulder, and ran the bow across the strings, checking the tuning. "But you have played for me. So, I will play for you."

His melody began, and it was as if the sounds of nature came from his music. Elin heard him mimic the chirping of birds, the whistling of wind. He improvised a tune that was joyful and free flowing, like the river's waves. And then his song became moodier, making her think of the night creeping over the land.

Elin had to remind herself to breathe as she listened, and leaned back to grip the edge of the table, needing something tangible to focus on. As her body came alive earlier, so did her spirit, his music dancing in her ears and through her head.

He lowered the instrument as she realized the fire was dying in the hearth. The only light in the cottage was the desperate sparks of embers and his aqua eyes, so blue they shone.

Fossegrimen set the fiddle on the table near her. Her body was mere inches away from his as he studied her trembling form. He swept a hand up to her cheek and moved his face toward hers. She closed her eyes, as her arms wrapped around his waist, and their lips met.

Liquid heat shot through her veins as he kissed her gently, his hand pressing against her back to steady her. His mouth parted moments later, and he tasted like cool mountain air and fresh water from snowmelt. The sensation was a shock to her system. When Elin brought herself to him two and a half weeks ago, she thought she had mentally prepared herself for this moment. She thought he would take her on the banks, with no regard for her comfort or desires, and she had come to terms with that.

Yet, with his careful touch and delicate kiss, she felt she was sacred to him in that moment. Urgency slipped through momentarily, when he took her hands from around his middle, and pressed them to the exposed skin of his chest.

"Feel me," he breathed, barely breaking their kiss. "Before I go...please..."

She explored his torso, feeling the hardness of his stomach, the stocky strength of his back, and the slight swell of muscle in his chest—the Viking build of her people. As her hands ran along his skin, his lips trailed down to her neck. He was walking her backward in the midst of all this, she realized, as the back of her legs hit what felt like the edge of her bed.

With that, his arms disappeared from around her body, and she fell back onto the mattress. She kept her eyes closed, waiting for his next actions—but nothing came. She sat up, and looked around. He was gone. All that remained of him was the smell of him on her skin, on her clothes.

She laid back on the covers, and sighed. Reaching up to unbutton her shirt, she decided to quell the desire descending between her legs—trying to ignore the pang of longing for him to finish the job.

*

Two days later Elin found herself at the riverbank, tuning her violin as she waited for him. Her fingertips danced over the neck of the fiddle, her bow flying across the strings. The other night had released something within her: an abandon and freeness with her music that she had never had before. She longed to show him the spark that had lit inside her—but he was late.

About two hours late.

She had found a dry rock to sit on, her skirt pulled up to her knees to keep it out of the water. Her elbow was beginning to feel cramped from holding her instrument as she played. The music was keeping doubtful thoughts at bay, those that had kept entering her mind the longer she waited. And then, something snapped within her.

Elin stood, feeling like a rock had been dropped on her chest. Realization hit her: the spirit had probably taken what he desired, and was leaving her to fend for herself. He'd decided that she wasn't what he wanted. Auditions were sixteen days away, and he was choosing to leave her during her most crucial time.

She kicked the water near the shore, letting out a scream and cursing in her native tongue.

"Faen ta deg!" Stomping over to the shore, she unlatched her violin case violently, and put her instrument inside. *"Faen i helvete!"*

She turned to the river, and approached it once more, dropping to her knees as a knot rose in her throat. "I'm so stupid," she whimpered. Tears fell from her eyes, down her cheeks, and into the waves. "Why did I think Fossegrimen would help me? Why? Why would I think a spirit would..."

Suddenly, there was the sound of water splashing, as though something was breaking through the surface of the river. Elin looked up, and three feet away from her, stood her mentor. His white shirt was buttoned up once more, sticking to his skin due to its wetness, and his soaked hair fell in thick strands on his shoulders.

His brow was furrowed, and his hands were clenched at his sides. She stood angrily, rolling her shoulders back, feeling heat behind her eyes as she glared at him. But still, she waited for him to explain himself.

"You don't need my lessons," he stated, his tone hard.

Elin pursed her lips, and took a step toward him. "What do you mean by *that*?"

"You don't need my lessons," he repeated. "And I am not going take a woman who is only offering herself in desperation." He turned, facing away from her, to gaze at the other side of the bank. "My own loneliness caused me to ignore my moral compass. You're not the first person who has come to me offering themselves as meat. And I doubt you'll be the last. But I swore to myself to never take someone so desperate up on that offer."

"I wouldn't have assumed you lived without such things, considering what happened the other night," she accused.

"I've had companionship from humans before, and it has never come to a good end. It is hard to see someone you care for go toward old age as you outlive them." He looked over his shoulder at her. "Do you think spirits don't come to crave, or come to care for, the people they are attracted to?" He ran a hand through his hair, taking a pause before continuing. "There is a reason the old women in your village still tell the stories of Fossegrimen. The elder ones knew, or their mothers knew, or their grandmothers knew."

"But they made a choice, fully knowing the outcome," Elin retorted. "You gave them the option to make that choice!"

He glided toward her, as though the stream was carrying him. "Are you telling me," he said, looking down at her, "that you would have given yourself to me freely if you were not desperate for what I could teach you?"

"I would have given you meat if I could afford to—" she began.

He laughed darkly. "So, I thought."

"—and would have given you myself of my own will, following my own desires."

Fossegrimen went silent, and the sad countenance left his face. He moved backward, deeper into the rill. "What?"

Her shoulders relaxed, and she walked toward him. "I know you heard me, River."

With each step, the water inched higher, until she was in front of him. The waves lapped around her thighs and without hesitancy, she kissed him.

He clasped his arms around her hungrily, and they fell back into the water. It was surprisingly warm, but that is not what shocked her. Elin realized that while holding onto him, she could *breathe* below the surface.

"My gift to you," his voice echoed inside her mind. Before she could ask questions, before *wondering* if she could talk underwater, he continued. *"Yes, you're actually hearing me. This communication only happens one way; I can't hear you if you try speaking to me like this. So, if you need to say anything or something is wrong, point toward the surface and I will swim up there. Now, do you want to continue? Nod, or point up."*

She answered by grabbing him for a kiss. He returned her touch with vigor, their tongues dancing, his hands moving across the topography of her body. Tentatively, he cupped her breast in his hand, and the warmth of his skin seeped through her layers of clothes. She reached up to unbutton her shirt, but he grabbed her wrist.

"No, if you let go of me...I can't risk my home chilling you. My powers protect you as long as you hold onto me."

Her impatience spoke for itself, as her hips pressed into his—and she felt his excitement, hard, unyielding for her. Suddenly, the current was carrying them somewhere, rushing them through the water, and moments later Fossegrimen pulled her up to the surface.

Instinctually, she sucked in air, her heart racing. She rubbed at her eyes, trying to acclimate to being above the water again. He held tight to her, giving her certainty in a world of new sensations.

"I have you," he soothed. "Take the time you need."

After a few moments, she looked around, to see they were in a cave. The stone walls, while grey, shimmered with sparkling minerals embedded in the walls. Lanterns on a nearby bank lit the cavern...and on that shore, she saw a simple table, two chairs, and a violin case sitting upon a small shelf.

"This is where I come to practice my craft," Fossegrimen explained. "This is an underwater cavern, containing an air pocket. As you know, I lose my form on land if I am far enough from my river, so I can bring companions here without such a fear."

With an arm around her, he helped Elin swim toward the sloping shore, which was a perfect incline for her to sit on dry ground, while he remained in the water. She pushed a few sopping strands of hair behind her shoulder, and looked around the cave smiling.

"This is incredible," she sighed.

"Thank you," Fossegrimen said, stepping out of the water. He moved past her, placing a kiss on her forehead as he did so, and grabbed the violin case on the table. He opened it, lifting a beautifully crafted hardanger fiddle from inside. Elin gasped. She had never seen anything like it. The fingerboard of the violin was abalone shell, and the etching on the body of the fiddle held intricate designs of river motifs.

"That's gorgeous," she said. "I have never seen a fiddle so beautifully crafted."

"And she plays just as lovely." He motioned toward her. "Come, we must have our lesson. I want to hear you play her, my dear."

*

About an hour later, Elin lifted the bow from the violin, letting the final note echo throughout the cave. The acoustics were glorious. The music she created bounced off the cave walls, surrounding her and Fossegrimen, enveloping them. She looked at him for approval. Sitting at the table, his head resting on his hand, he was smiling at her, his gaze full of adoration.

"They will think they are hearing the music of God," he said, standing from the chair. "Your audition will leave the church in awe. You read sheet music, correct?"

She nodded. "My father taught me. I can sight read well."

He walked toward her, reaching out to cup her face in his hand. "You'll be a triumph."

After taking the violin from her, he set it on the table, and wrapped his arms around her waist. "I have to take you back. It will be sun rise in a few hours."

"I can sleep throughout today," she said. "Not yet. Let us have more time."

He bent down, his lips brushing against the top of her head. "Elin..."

She reached up to the buttons of his shirt, and after undoing them, kissed the skin above his heart. A low growl emanated from his throat, and his grip tightened at her back.

"You left me longing the other night," she confessed.

"Did I?"

She nodded, trailing her kisses down to his stomach. He lifted her to his chest, and walked backwards toward the water, taking her with him. He laid her down on the slope of the bank, their lower halves in the water.

"Then tonight," he whispered, his lips circling her ear, "I won't leave you unfulfilled."

"And how do you plan on doing that?"

He grinned. "With my mouth, if you'll let me."

Her brows lifted. "Oh, you're not going to...?"

"No," he said, shaking his head. "Not tonight, not in my domain. If the time comes for that, it will be in bed, and things will be proper—"

"What do you mean proper?"

He kissed her silent. "You'll know soon. But for right now, I want to show you, to teach you."

His hands moved to her chest, his thumb and pointer finger applying delightful pressure to her nipples through the fabric of her dress. Despite the layers of her skirt and his trousers, she felt him hard against her thighs. She reached down daringly, and placed a palm over him. He jumped slightly at her touch, but after a moment, his hips pushed into her hand.

"Gently," he instructed. "Like how you hold the neck of a fiddle. You don't choke it. You can grip me firmly, but gently."

She reached under his waistband, and did as he described. He gasped. "Yes, yes like that."

He felt smooth and unyielding in her hand. She worked him up and down, trying to remember what she had read in books and attempting to maneuver things based on his reactions. His hands left her chest, searching under her skirt, giving her an indicator she was doing things correctly.

"Have you felt someone's fingers inside you?" He asked.

"Only my own."

"Then, may I?"

"Yes."

With a rustling of fabric, and his hand skimming her thighs for a moment, he carefully felt her entrance, before sliding one finger inside her, then two. Her hands were smaller than his, and she was unaccustomed to such girth, evident by her body's slight resistance.

"If this is too much we can stop," he reassured.

"No, I want to keep going."

He kissed her, and slowly moved his digits in and out of her, his fingertips tilted up to touch the most sensitive part of her inner walls. His thumb gently rubbed her clitoris, curiously matching the rhythm of his movements with how she stroked him.

She sighed, feeling in a curious way that she was his instrument, as he pressed against her inside like she was delicate violin strings, and he was trying to discover her song. Her cheeks reddened with that thought: of him being the master of his craft—of her for a moment.

His fingers then retreated from her, and he sat up. He maneuvered himself between her legs, lifting her skirt and layers to her waist. "May I drink from you, Elin?"

"Yes."

He bent down, lowering his mouth to her entrance. He kissed her inner thighs, his tongue dancing up her skin with warmth and wetness. Moments later, a gentle kiss was placed on her folds, and then his tongue parted that delicate skin. She gasped, and his head shot up.

"Is this all right?"

Letting out a chuckle, she answered. "Yes, just new. I will verbally tell you if I am uncomfortable."

He nodded, giving a smile before going back down. His tongue continued his tentative exploration, probing and teasing. With the tip, he gently licked her clitoris, and she moaned. She felt a jolt of heat run up her spine, and her hips lifted toward his mouth.

That seemed to encourage him as he focused on that bundle of nerves. He hummed, the vibrations hitting her delightfully. She reached down, and dug her hand in his hair, keeping him close to her as she neared her crescendo.

For the first time, someone else brought her climax to her. As her body shook beneath his hold, she felt his fingers lace between her free ones, and she held tight. Her body rocked back and forth, while his tongue lapped up her last few drops of pleasure. A few moments passed before she came back down from whatever mythical place his touch had taken her.

Fossegrimen had lifted himself from her, studying her as she regained her senses.

"You were glorious," he said. "Wonderfully glorious."

"Thank you," she sighed. "As were you."

He gathered her in his arms, pulling her to his chest. "I think it's time we get you home, my darling."

*

The next week flew like the wind. Elin took to practicing like usual, counting down the days until the auditions with the church. She had a final Thursday lesson with Fossegrimen, and then the next Monday were the auditions. Word had gotten back to her that all three fiddle players in town were still set to audition—but had become unnerved about her developing talent that they had seen in the past few weeks. Her performances in town had made her improvement in skill quite clear, and she felt a newfound power making the menfolk quake in their boots.

The Wednesday before her final lesson with Fossegrimen, she walked into town to simply shop. She decided to practice behind closed doors and not reveal the extent of her skill until the audition. A basket hung off her arm as she walked from shop keep to shop keep, filling it with what she needed for the upcoming week. Thread for fixing her clothes, a lump of cheese and bread for meals, and mint tea for a relaxing evening tuck in.

As she exited the baker's store, she looked across the town square to see Grete straightening up her flower stand. The elderly woman, even in her late sixties, still tended her gardens herself—and it was evident with her hearty and vibrant blooms. Elin waved to her, and she waved back, her usual friendly smile on her weathered face.

But then, Grete's expression seemed to drop for a moment, gazing at Elin. She lifted a silver strand of hair from her eyes, tucking it back into her bun, and motioned toward the young woman. "Come here, child! I haven't seen you for a while!"

Elin hurried to her, stopping short of the flower stand's counter. Behind it, stood Grete, surrounded by pots of water with flowers of all sorts. lily of the valley, white dryad, primrose, and pennywort meshed together in a colorful collage of hues and sweet smells that was almost dizzying.

"These are beautiful, Grete," Elin said, taking her calloused hands. "No one grows buds like you."

"My grandson is starting to," she chuckled, her voice sounding rich, sweet, and deep like warm cider. "He helps his mother in the gardens now. I think next spring, I will simply direct them in the work instead of getting in the dirt myself."

She paused for a moment. "I saw your bouquet you left at my father's grave. Foxglove was always his favorite. Thank you."

"How did you know they were my flowers?"

"No one else can grow flowers like you, Grete. Everyone can tell your blooms from the rest."

She gave a toothy grin. "I just wish I could have left flowers sooner. The winter lasted a little longer than expected, but I swore that the first foxglove would be your papa's." She gave her hands a gentle squeeze. "I've been listening to you play in the square. Arvid would be so proud of you. You have really grown as a musician, Elin."

She beamed. "I am just hoping the church will be as impressed as you."

"I know they will be." Grete placed a hand under her chin. "Fossegrimen has taught you well."

Elin's eyes widened, and she felt as though glass was shattering in her brain. Her stomach was doing backflips, as her hands slipped out of Grete's. "Pardon me?"

"Now, now, your secret is safe with me and the other elders," Grete soothed. She wiped her hands on her blue skirt, embroidered with flowers as dazzling as her natural ones. "We women know the signs of one under his tutelage. But of course, your situation is slightly different, isn't it?"

"I don't know what you mean..."

"Yes, you do, but of course, these matters are private. I understand. Just know, you don't need to feel shame about what has occurred. Your choices are your own. It has been about two generations since he showed his favor to one, but a lot of us remember the accounts. Some of us—even remember our own experiences."

Grete looked at her knowingly, and then turned to her flowers, gathering various hues of primroses before handing the small bundle to Elin. "Put these in water, and when he visits you tomorrow night, wear them in your hair. River always loved to see flowers in one's hair." She patted her head lovingly. "But you'd know all this, and would have been more prepared, if you'd *visit Grete more*. Don't be a stranger to my booth, young lady."

Elin smiled. "Okay, I won't. Thank you, Grete." She reached into her pocket to fish out some coin, but Grete put a hand on her arm.

"Those flowers are my gift to you. I give those to all who have such an experience with River. As well as this." It was then Grete pulled out a small fabric bag from her apron, and pressed it into Elin's palm. "Tell no one I gave you this."

She loosened the drawstring, and peered inside. The bag held about a dozen or so teabags, and she looked at Grete quizzically. "What is this?"

"Raspberry and parsley tea. Drink one cup each morning, after you are *with* him, until all the bags are gone. You can add sugar or honey if it is bitter. If you have any complications or questions, come see me."

She set the bag in her basket, nodding. "I understand. Thank you."

*

Elin stood in front of her reflection in the window, carefully tucking primroses in her braided crown of hair. It had taken her about an hour to French braid and pin her hair, but she was pleased with the results. She ran her finger tips around the circle of entwined hair, feeling as though she looked like Tatiana, the famed fae queen.

Before turning from the window, she pinched her cheeks to add some color to her face, and strode over to her violin case on the table.

Before she could grab it and head toward the river, there was a knock at her door.

She knew it was him; she could feel it in her bones. With a deep breath, she answered the door, and Fossegrimen stood before her. And like her, it seemed he too had dressed for the occasion. While his trousers and boots remained the same, his upper half was quite different. He wore a double-breasted black vest, with a grey button down underneath, a tie, and a dark jacket over it all. A silver pocket watch chain peeked out from the opening of the jacket, running across his waist.

She opened her mouth to compliment him, but he beat her to the punch.

He touched the flowers in her braid. "Hello, my beautiful protegee."

She smiled. "Good evening, my handsome maestro. I was on my way to you."

"I knew you were. But I wanted to come to you tonight, to make up for my lateness last week." He stepped inside, and after she shut the door, he leaned down to kiss her. "Put your violin away. We won't need it tonight."

She blinked at him in surprise, but did as he asked. "Why, Fossegrimen?"

"You know I can't be away too long from the river. I did some things to prepare for tonight, but my time is still limited, and I don't want to rush..." His voice trailed off, and he took a step back. "I'm sorry, I shouldn't have assumed that we would—I mean, I shouldn't..."

"I want this too." She wrapped her arms around him. "I want you."

"Do you? Are you sure?"

"Yes."

He daringly grabbed her hips, holding her to him, his lips crashing into hers. With quick hands, he reached toward the front lacing of her dress, and with skilled fingers, untied the ribbon and began loosening it. In the same turn, she impatiently tugged at his jacket, sliding it off his arms and tossing it onto the chair.

Her fingers ran down the silver buttons of his vest, right as he lowered the top part of her dress, exposing her chest. Taking a few steps back, he gazed at her naked torso, and reached out with a careful touch to fondle her breast.

To her surprise, his pawing only lasted a moment, before he quickly unfastened his vest and shirt, casting it aside to join the jacket on the chair. Again, he pulled her to him, at last achieving skin to skin contact.

"This is what I've wanted, more than anything," he sighed into her hair.

"I think I felt the same way," she whispered. "I want to lie naked with you, River. Just for a moment, nothing else."

"I think I'd like that too."

While kissing down her body, he eased her dress over her hips, finally seeing her fully naked before him. For a moment he explored her, his palms skimming over the swell of her belly and then to feel the strength of her thighs. After a while, he fell to his knees, his mouth level with her quim, and his tongue began their ministrations that delighted her the other night.

She bent forward slightly, gripping his shoulders to steady herself. Yet her legs almost completely gave out when he groaned, "You taste like nectar, my darling. Such a lovely chalice that gives me sweet wine..."

He seemed to sense her shakiness, for he parted from her, and after standing, gathered her in his arms. He carried her toward the bed and set her upon it, before reaching down to undo his trousers and slip them off. Elin stared, gazing at his legs that were as toned as his torso. Everything about him was truly stocky, hard—including what was between his legs.

Fossegrimen laid down beside her, and took her face in his hands. His thumb grazed across her bottom lip, and he reached up to her hair as he always did, to let it loose around her shoulders and chest.

"You're beautiful," he sighed. "You're breathtaking."

"As are you," she said, tilting her head to kiss him.

As he embraced her, she reached down to stroke him, and he let out a groan. Feeling mischievous, she parted her legs slightly, and let the tip of him brush up against her entrance, and then held it to her clitoris. Her hips moved, delightfully rubbing that bundle of nerves against him.

"Elin," he gasped. "Elin, do you want to do this?"

"I'm ready, River."

Her hand released him, and he carefully maneuvered himself so he was above her. He rested his weight on his forearms, giving her space and the ability to adjust herself comfortably below.

"Let me know if you need me to stop," he said. "You can say no at any point, and I promise, I will stop."

"I know. I trust you."

He put her forehead to hers. "Just remember to keep breathing, and relax."

With that, he reached down to angle himself at her entrance, and then—he gently pushed forward.

It did feel strange, having someone else enter her for the first time. She gasped, feeling her inner walls stretch for him. For a second, her body tightened, and only then did it slightly hurt.

"Elin, breathe into it," Fossegrimen soothed. "Breathe, my lover." He didn't move as she inhaled deeply, and allowed herself to slowly exhale. "Do I need to stop?"

"No!" She protested. "Please don't, I want to know."

He inched forward again, and with her breathing, her body was able to relax. In fact, she marveled at her natural ability to accommodate his size—and that the more he filled her, the more he was able to caress certain points of sensitivity.

At last, he filled her to the hilt, beads of sweat on the side of his face, and his hands gripping the sheets beside her.

"River?" She reached up to touch his face. "Are *you* all right?"

"Honestly, you just feel that good Elin. I am trying to pace myself and be gentle with you." She laughed, and he placed a hand on her hip. "Damn, it—it feels interesting when you laugh."

"A good interesting?"

He smiled, kissing the side of her face. "A wonderful interesting."

At that moment, he began to rock back and forth within her, and she shuddered. He felt so, so good. Her body instinctually met his movements, her hips rolling into his. When her right leg hooked around him, that gave each of them the signal they could stop worrying, and enjoy their connection.

He bent his head down to lick her cleavage, and to bury his face in her chest. In the meantime, her hands roamed down his back to the defined muscles of his buttocks. Playfully, she gripped them, and he growled into her skin.

In response, she reached up to grab his hair, pull it back, and kiss him. He groaned, grinding himself deeper within her. She could feel her insides coiling, her feelings mounting within. With each stroke, the base of him hit her clit, causing a pulse of pleasure each time.

"I can feel you," he sighed. "Elin, let go for me. Please." He leaned down, whispering in her ear. "Share with me your secret song; play for your mentor."

"River," she groaned. "River..."

"I don't want to hold back anymore, my love. Please!"

That was when, at last, her body threw itself over the peak of her orgasm. She screamed, shaking as wave after wave of euphoria hit her. During this time, she felt him quicken his movement, an effort to prolong her pleasure, and then...

"I-I can't hold back, Elin...Elin!"

He cried out her name as he finished, briefly meeting her in her moment of rapture. She could feel him fill her, as she came back down from her high. There was a brief moment, where his forehead was to hers, and his shaking arms did their best to hold her. He rolled off her carefully, to lay on his side, and pull her to his chest.

"How was that for you?" He asked softly.

She looked up at him. "It was exactly what I wanted."

"Is there anything you want me to do next time?"

"You want to see me again?"

He nodded. "For as long as you'd let me. Elin, I would like to court you."

Her heart skipped a beat. "What?"

"I would like to court you."

"I need to think about that," she said, truthfully. "I never imagined my life would involve companionship. I do care for you, but I need to get through the audition and..."

"I don't need an answer right now," he soothed. "I just wanted to let you know of my intentions and desires. Any sort of courtship can be on our terms as well. I know you aren't one for tradition. And even if you say no, I wouldn't harbor any negative feelings."

She smiled. "You will always have my friendship too, if you'd accept that."

"Always, Elin."

*

Elin sat in the pew of the church, listening as Robert finished his solo. He was the last fiddler to go, before it was her turn to take to the front of the sanctuary and impress her "judges": the choir/music director and the pastor. Gripping her violin nervously, she remembered to breathe deep and slow. The night before she had walked to the river, fiddle in hand, for one last session before the audition. For most of it, Fossegrimen reassured her of her skill—and in between exercises and songs, distracted her with kisses.

At last, Robert lowered his fiddle, and took a bow as those in the pews clapped. About twenty of the town's people had come to listen to the auditions, for the church was always open to all. The pastor, a wizened man in his forties, thanked Robert as he sat back down with his family, who had shown up in support.

It was then Elin was called to proceed with her audition, and quiet gasps echoed in the sanctuary. She wished she had people there for her at that moment, but she knew that in the past, she'd had to do the hardest things in her life alone. Walking up to the pulpit, someone from the pew up front whispered to her, "Elin!"

She glanced over to see it was Grete, hands clasped in front of her, beaming. Flashing the old florist a subtle smile, she climbed the few steps to the front of the church, and looked up at the balcony. To her surprise, there was a single figure leaning against the railing, looking down at her. Due to the sun coming through the stained glass, Elin couldn't see too clearly, but he appeared to have long hair trailing down his shoulders, and wore a white button down with black trousers.

"Whenever you are ready, Elin," the pastor said.

Wordlessly, bringing her father's Hardanger fiddle to her shoulder, she lowered her bow on the strings and began to play.

Epilogue

Elieen looked at her dress one more time in the hotel mirror. She was pleased with the off the shoulder, midnight blue evening gown. For a quick grab off the *Macy's* clearance rack, it would do for a Broadway opening night. With her hair pinned in a smart looking updo, she was able to show off the diamond earrings that Lucas had given her as a two-year anniversary present. She couldn't believe that time had flown so quickly.

She decided to wear those and her wedding ring for the event. Sighing, Elieen wished that James could have made it to the show, but alas a business trip had called him away. Even though theater wasn't exactly his thing, her husband did feel guilty for missing the opening night of Lucas' new musical, *Requiem for an Aria*, and had sent Lucas a congratulatory box of cigars. Eileen smiled, remembering how Lucas sat on the hotel room balcony smoking one after making love to her.

Moments later, she spritzed on a bit of perfume and checked to see if her credit card, room key, lipstick, and cellphone were in her black clutch. With that, she slipped into silver kitten heels and made her way to Riya's room to see if she and Kyden were ready to catch their Uber for dinner.

*

"Are you sure this looks okay?" Kyden asked.

Riya assessed the man-bun one more time, and nodded. "I think you totally pull it off," she answered.

He touched it uncertainly. "If you say so."

"If you aren't sure babe, you can take it out. It would look good in a braid too."

"No, no. If you say it looks good, I trust you."

She walked over to him and straightened his burgundy tie. Riya thought her boyfriend looked good in just about anything, but the slate grey suit just made his eyes pop. In one graceful moment, his hand swept to her cheek, tilting her face up for a kiss.

"You're gorgeous," he said, his fangs playfully pricking her bottom lip.

"Down boy. We *do not* have time. Elieen is going to be here any moment so we can catch our ride."

"Of course, my love."

She smoothed out her blood red dress, and walked over to the bed to fasten her gold heels. She had pinned her hair back behind her ears with ruby and gold clips, a gift from Kyden for her first red carpet event.

"It will be strange being on the other side of the camera," he admitted. "I have done interviews before for exhibitions, but nothing like this."

"I can't believe we get to walk the red carpet."

"Yeah. The closest I have gotten is doing photography for *Paris Fashion Week*."

"Maybe it's a combination of you being the photographer for *Requiem's* promo, or—"

"Or Elieen being the second partner of Lucas Acosta. This is her first public appearance with him, and I think he wanted us to be there for support."

Riya took a deep breath. "Yeah, probably. But I am so proud of them. I think everyone going public about being polyamorous is so brave. I'm just glad they got to announce it on social media on their own terms."

"Veronica's statement online was honestly beautiful."

"I *love* Lucas' wife. And the picture she posted with her girlfriend was so cute."

"That woman is a wizard with lighting. Beach pictures can be a *bitch* on a cell phone camera."

At that moment there was a knock on the door and Kyden hurried over to answer it. "Eileen, you look stunning!"

Riya turned to see her best friend walk into the hotel room, a vision in blue. "Oh my god," she gasped. "That dress was truly a find, girl."

"Thank you. You look amazing too, both of you." Eileen sized up the couple as Riya walked over to Kyden. "You look like a power couple."

"That's because we are a power couple," Kyden said, kissing her cheek.

"Gross. Anyway, you two ready?"

Riya nodded. "Yeah, I think so."

Eileen glanced at Kyden. "Are you sure you're comfortable coming to dinner with us?"

"I will have the usual glass of wine and soup."

"Soup?"

Riya sighed. "He just sips the broth. He can have liquids, just not solids."

"Sorry I—I am still getting used to the vampire thing." Eileen blushed, nervously fingering her wedding band.

"It's only been three months. You're doing great," he reassured.

"Much better than when you chucked a cross at him and yelled, 'Back demon!'" Riya laughed.

"Yeah well—telling me while I was housesitting for my *religious mother* wasn't the greatest idea." They then heard a notification go off on Eileen's phone, and she whipped it out. "The Uber is here! Let's go. Lucas and his brother are already on their way to the restaurant."

*

Camille could feel herself vibrating with excitement. She couldn't believe that she and Alex were attending the opening night of *Requiem for an Aria*—and that her best friend was in the cast. Camille wished that she could go back in time to her and Leah's childhood selves, and tell them that the hard work, tears, and creation through challenge would be all worth it one day.

"I am so excited!" Camille said, looking at Alexander. "I never imagined I would be walking a red carpet."

"You better get used to it," he chuckled, kissing her hand. "It will probably happen again with *In the Middle of Somewhere*. You'll have to be by my side, considering I wrote that play because of you."

"How are the edits going for it?"

"I got a lot of really good notes from the last workshop. I think it's almost ready."

She looked out the car window, gazing up at the New York skyline. "I know Leah is really nervous about tonight."

"She's a strong chorus member. She's got this."

"I agree. And I think being in the chorus is a perfect introduction to the Broadway stage."

"She has a lot of promise. This is a good test run for her."

"*Requiem for an Aria* has such beautiful music. There's going to be a bunch of choir students attempting to sing the songs once the cast recording comes out."

"Lucas is a damn good composer. I have a gut feeling; this is going to be the next hit show. I just feel it in my bones, Camille."

At that moment the uber arrived at the restaurant, and Alexander reached over to take Camille's hand. He squinted at the front entrance to see Lucas with Veronica on one side, and a woman with blonde hair, wearing a blue dress on the other.

"Looks like Elieen arrived. Riya and Kyden must be inside," he murmured.

"Okay, let me make sure I got this right," Camille said. "Eileen is dating Lucas and Riya is Elieen's best friend? And Kyden is the photographer who took pictures of the show and happens to be dating Riya?"

"You got it."

She laughed. "*Finally*. Polyamory is confusing."

Alexander shrugged. "I wouldn't do it, but Veronica and him seem happy."

"Oh God, is Veronica's girlfriend going to be here too?"

"No, she's having celebratory drinks with her friends. Big events make her nervous."

"I need a flowchart for all this"

The uber came to a stop, and Alexander opened the door. He got out of the car, and offered Camille a hand. "Ready for a wonderful evening, my love?"

She nodded with a smile. "I'm ready."

*

Leah was hyperventilating backstage. She leaned against the brick wall; thankful she was able to be alone before most of the cast arrived. She had shown up an hour and a half before curtain, just to have some time alone in the space. Opening nights had always wrecked her emotionally, and thanks to past incidents, she knew to arrive early to a theater to have her ceremonial freak-out.

But this anxiety attack was bad, and she knew it. Her hands were shaking, and the salad she had eaten a few hours ago felt like it was ricocheting against her insides. She slid down onto the floor and tried to do her deep breathing exercises.

"I thought I heard someone back here," a familiar voice said.

Leah looked up, to see it was Tove Pedersen, first violinist of the orchestra. She was wearing a black lace dress with high boots, something out of step with her usual attire of jeans and a t-shirt. Tove and Leah had become close during rehearsals for *Requiem for an Aria*. During breaks they often gravitated toward each other, and had begun hanging out outside of the theater as well. Tove, who had been in New York for the past five years, had taken it upon herself to be Leah's guide to the city.

Tove sat down next to her, and brushed a strand of hair from Leah's face. "Let me guess: first Broadway show freakout?"

Leah sniffled, tears gathering in her eyes. "Yeah."

"I went through the same thing when I was in my first performance," she soothed. "It's been eleven years, and I still have shows where I get worked up. It's normal to feel like this."

"Yeah, but you were a goddamn prodigy," Leah whimpered. "You started performing in orchestras when you were *sixteen*. I am a twenty-six-year-old just now having a major break..."

"In a *Lucas Acosta* musical. You know that's a big deal."

"What if he only cast me because my best friend is his brother's *fucking girlfriend*?" Tove flicked the side of her head. "Hey!"

"Well now you're just *å være dum*. You know you didn't get cast because of nepotism. I have worked with Lucas on shows before, and he would *never*." Tove sighed. "*Se*, I know Broadway shows are a different beast than other productions. Coming here from Norway was a huge shock to me. But Leah, you deserve to be here. You've told me how hard you've worked for this. Please try to be in the moment. Savor this. And remember...we party tonight!"

Leah laughed a little, and wiped the tears off her cheeks. "You have been a rock to me since I came here, Tove. Thank you."

It was then Tove's phone buzzed in her pocket, and she glanced at it, smiling.

"A dress with pockets? Nice!" Leah said.

"I *know* right? I found it at a thrift store. This is my usual opening night dress." Trove stood, and offered her hand to help Leah up. "Come on. I want you to meet my grandfather. He's at the stage door. I forgot my water bottle at the apartment and he brought it for me."

"He was able to make it to opening night?" Leah asked.

"Yeah, he caught an earlier flight out of Norway. He's staying with me for the rest of the week."

"I would be thrilled to meet him. He's the one who first taught you how to play the violin, right?"

"Yes! The *maestro* himself!"

They made their way backstage to the outside door, and out in the alley, Leah saw a man in his early forties leaning against the theater, Tove's emerald green metal water bottle in hand. She blinked. Surely this man wasn't Tove's grandfather? He looked more like he could be her dad. Yes, there was some grey at his temples and beard, but his face looked *so young*. He still had a full head of dark brown, wavy hair pulled back into a ponytail. He wore fitted slacks, suspenders, and a sky-blue button down that made his eyes look vibrant. He smiled playfully at Tove, shaking his head. They had the same smile and eye color, Leah realized. The family resemblance was *definitely* there.

"Pling i bollen," he chuckled.

"I know, I know, I'm a space case," Tove sighed, striding over to him. She took the water bottle and gave him a hug. "Thank you, Grandfather." She backed away, and motioned toward Leah.

"Leah, this is my grandfather," she said. "Grandpa, this is Leah Bell."

"Ah, you're the friend that Tove told me about," he noted, speaking with a lilt of a Norwegian accent. "It's so nice to finally meet you. Call me River."

As Leah stepped toward him, she noted around his neck, a chain with a small bottle as a pendant. Inside appeared to be a clear liquid of some sort.

"The pleasure is mine," she said. "I really like your necklace."

"Thank you, my dear. It's from a river near my house. I like having a bit of my home wherever I may go."

"I'm glad you could get it past the TSA," Tove laughed. "It's a bitch here."

"You know I have my ways," he said, waving a hand in the air.

"Speaking of ways..." she began. "Grandfather, maybe you could help Leah with something. You know how you used to calm me down before my performances? I think Leah could use a little bit of that magic right now."

River gave a warm smile to Leah. "Nervous about your Broadway debut?"

She nodded. "Yeah."

"That's completely natural. Here, if it is all right, give me your hands."

She held them out, and he took them in his gentle grasp. His grip felt warm and oddly soothing, as though his heat penetrated her skin. "Now close your eyes." She did as he asked. "Okay, take a few deep breaths with me and listen to my voice..."

*

The crowd was thunderous as the cast took another bow. Eileen wiped at the tears gathering in her eyes, careful to not ruin her makeup. Lucas had told her the history of Charlotte DeLaney and her secret romance with her mysterious masked partner, but there was nothing like seeing it unfold through music and the stage. She had a feeling, with Charlotte's legacy as an operatic star who had a flair for the dramatic on and off stage—she would have approved of her love story being narrated in such a way.

Eileen had found it beautiful that, despite the confinement of culture which prevailed during DeLaney's life, she chose to have a decades-long relationship that was on her terms. Even with the press hounding her for her partner's identity, she never let the world know. Sniffling dramatically next to her was Riya, who stood in ovation with her and the rest of the audience.

"This show is going to be a *hit*," Kyden said, as the house lights came up.

"The costuming, the sets—it all felt so rich without being too much," Riya noted.

"It was such a fun musical to photograph for that reason," he admitted.

"God, I feel emotionally *wrecked*."

"I know," Eileen said. "Like, when Charlotte paid off that sleazy photographer to not release the photos of her lover...I am still destroyed over that scene."

"They just wanted a happy life, where they could be accepted."

"A lot of those themes hold true today," Kyden sighed.

Eileen smiled. "To see Lucas on that stage—taking that bow with the cast. It made me think of all that. I feel lucky that we don't have to hide like they did. To have the *privilege* to not hide."

"His name reveal at the end was *so good too*," Riya said. "She approved *him* to write her obituary; the only person who she felt ever knew her—Erique."

"Charlotte made sure she, and their legendary love, would live on."

Eileen felt her best friend put a hand on her shoulder. "Hey, we can analyze the show later. Are you ready to dance the night away with your man?"

She nodded, smiling. "I think I am."

"Come on then," Kyden said. "Let's go. We have an after party to catch!"

###

About the Author

Callixta/Calix King is an autistic, queer, and bi-gender artist living in the Kansas City, Missouri area. They attended college at Wichita State University and hold a degree in creative writing and theater. When they aren't trying to create some sort of eloquent narrative (or bang their head into their keyboard as an attempt to do so), they sing karaoke, write poetry), and enjoy a quiet cottagecore life. If you want to learn more about Callixta/Calix King (and see pictures of their adorable cats) follow them on Bluesky (https://bsky.app/profile/ckingwrites.bsky.social) and check out their personal website (https://www.ckingwrites.com).

www.ingramcontent.com/pod-product-compliance
Lightning Source LLC
Chambersburg PA
CBHW021215160726
47994CB00001B/489